J GORDON SMITH

THE BLUE CRYSTAL

A Novel of Swords, Sorcery
... & Dragons

Gemstone Series: Book IV

By:
J GORDON SMITH

Epic Swords & Sorcery

Ayton & Greene Publishing Company
Detroit, Michigan
Copyright (c) 2013, 2014 by J Gordon Smith

Dedication

To those old friends like Mark, Mike, and Matt who remained interested in the series during the very first drafts of the first book and encouraged continuing.

To those new friends and fans who have come to enjoy the rest of the broad epic of this ancient world. You keep me going.

Copyright

THE BLUE CRYSTAL
Copyright © 2013, 2014 by J Gordon Smith
All rights reserved. No part of this book may be used or reproduced in any manner without written permission except for brief quotations in critical articles or reviews.
Published globally by J Gordon Smith with Ayton & Greene Publishing Company

Official Author Website: http://jgordonsmith.com/

Cover Art & Book Design: Ayton & Greene Publishing Company
Map Art: J Gordon Smith
[Reference file #: GS4_Blue_Crystal_131208]

This is a work of fiction and intended for entertainment. The work may contain excessive violence or sexual situations that may not be suitable for some readers. All characters, names, places, incidents, and situations appearing in this work are imaginary or are used fictitiously. Any resemblance to actual events, locales, businesses, companies, or persons; living, dead, undead, mythical, or magical is purely and entirely coincidental.

Editorial Summary

Tyric dropped to his knees, his helmet sliding from his slack fingers, "She can't be dead!" He pressed his hands against the dragon's body. Nothing stirred. The fire in her eyes flickered and faded. "What am I to do?"

For a thousand years, the fair Enkarian Elves concealed secrets that threaten the land. Evil monsters and magic long thought lost to legend and myth have returned to fight a forgotten War. Now the Elves negotiate a desperate alliance in exchange for dark wizardry.

Can the blacksmith Tyric trust truths told by the insane Elf King of a mystical Dragon's Egg lost since the old War? A secret the King never shared with his two sons who both scheme for his throne? Will Tyric unearth his doom fulfilling the King's quest? Or will he find death from the silent weapons of the Rubied Assassins who hunt him? Should he trust the enchanting, yet secretive and dangerous woman, Anika? Will Tyric understand how his Destiny, and the mystical blue gem he carries, fit in the coming War – before it is too late to save those he loves?

Find out in THE BLUE CRYSTAL, Book 4 of the Gemstone Series.

Other Books Published in the Gemstone Series:
The Diamond Coronal
The Black Jewel
The Fire Gem

Official Author web blog:
J Gordon Smith   http://jgordonsmith.com

Map of the World

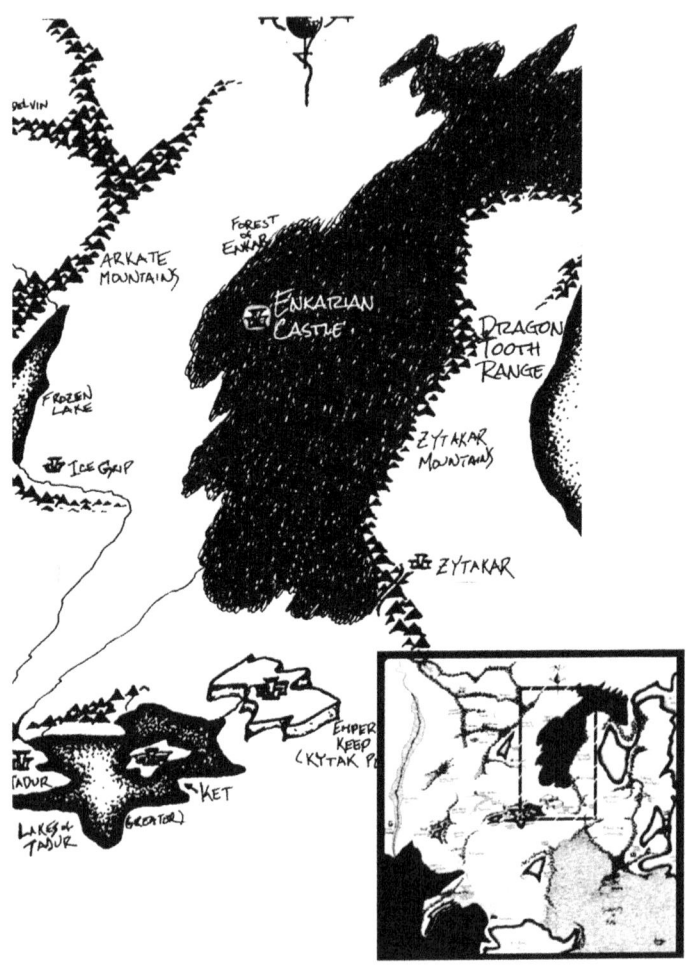

Chapter I: Forge Fire Tree

*"Stand Tall against the Shadows
for they cannot overcome,
a Heart that is Pure" - King Aleron*

*T*HWOQUE!

TYRIC SWUNG HIS AX INTO THE WOOD. The ax remained light in his hands thickened by years of swinging the forge hammer. His over-sized shoulders tightened, bringing the blade about quick and sure. Vibrations rippled along the black trunk like a stone thrown in a brook . Dried leaves that still clung to its branch tips swung with the mournful motions of the shredded standards left by dead kings upon a forgotten battlefield. Even the soggy black ground under his toes undulated when he struck the tree.

THWOQUE!

His ax gnawed deeper into the wood. Liberated patches of bark flaked off with each stroke revealing slivered bits of white fibers underneath. His pace remained methodical as he cut into the heart wood. His ax clove viscously, recalling the clack of long oars paced by a booming war drum. Strong, sharp, and incessant. A lesser ax could never cut the hard wood inside but

Tyric had forged this ax with magic, gaining the tattoo runes that embroidered his arms through that work.

THWOQUE!

The sound echoed across the greening forest that obscured most of the sky with new leaves, but the elvish forge fire tree stood alone with Tyric. The tree forcefully claimed its part of the forest. A stout tree that warred underground with its roots against encroaching predators. The other trees soared high overhead but they dare not approach the forge fire tree. Their limbs bowed away and allowed the strong moonlight to penetrate deep to the forest floor and burnish the ground around the tree.

THWOQUE!

Tyric paused to press the sweat from his brows. He wiped his hand on his heavy wool trousers and again gripped the oak shaft of his two headed ax. He had wrapped the handle in coarse canvas soaked in tree gum so it remained perpetually tactile. Elvish runes stretched around the shaft in a woven web of script that continued upon the steel.

Only after weeks of careful search did he locate the source of this tree's seed pods floating under their gossamer strands across the forest canopy. The magic in the tree would last in the fire for years enhancing any weapon forged by a blacksmith who learned to bend its power. The tree had its dangers though.

THWOQUE!

Light blazed free of the tree upon the clean face of the ax as more wood split apart. Motes of colorful dew drops danced from the widening wound. The little lights floated around the trunk in swirling groups, playful even, before him. He kept his eyes averted and focused on his task. Those lights mesmerized and eventually he would starve and nourish the roots of the tree. Its few defenses against the animals that walked the world.

THWOQUE!

His two oxen gurgled and chomped on their cud. Their tails slapped their legs against buzzing insects. The elves that had adopted him never had much use for draft animals, living under the forest trees, but these animals showed their worth when logging wood for his forge.

THWOQUE!

A dry branch snapped paces behind him. Tyric's ears had remained somehow clear in the years he lived with the forge fires and the ringing anvils. His thoughts weighed that sound. It was more than a bird and from an opposite side of the oxen. He swung his ax.

THWOQUE!

A sword whistled in the air toward him. Tyric used his backward ax swing to twist his body around and meet the sword with the flat of his ax.

The weapons rang against each other. Tyric spun his ax head about the shaft where the ax crescent locked into the sword and wedged it against the shaft. Tyric pulled and the basket guard on the sword nearly ripped his attackers thumb off at the knuckle joint.

Tyric spun his ax to kick the sword around where he snatched it from the air. His thick fingers filled the basket guard but a blink of his trained eye showed the sword would be serviceable.

The conflict somehow fed the tree or it sensed the possibility for sustenance filling its hunger instead of saving itself. New motes spit from pores in the wood up and down the trunk. They burst around Tyric but he had spun to face the menacing band of eight individuals arrayed before him with swords drawn. One figure held back from the rest and Tyric knew he needed to pay special attention to that one. He was dressed in better clothes than the others, steel where they had leather, leather where they had wool.

The first attacker, that lost his sword, threw a dagger. Tyric turned aside and beat the dagger from the air with the sword. He swung his ax at the next nearing attacker who winced back free of its edge. Tyric conserved the swing by carrying the arc of his ax up, around, and down splitting the third attacker from shoulder to hip before sufficient bone slowed the hammer power behind Tyric's arm. He shook the body from the ax and stabbed the first attacker with the sword. His boot kick lifted the second attacker and flipped him back into the fourth. Tyric drove forward like a trampling war horse and ran his sword through both of those downed attackers. The way clear, Tyric saw the attacker in the back motioning his hands in magic that Tyric recognized. Tyric threw his ax so it embedded in the wizard's body. The ax's runes readable on the farthest side of the wizard's spine as the body pitched forward.

Tyric turned and caught another sword against his borrowed weapon. The attacker's long dagger hit Tyric's chain mail like a punch to his ribs. Tyric backhanded his fist into the attacker's cheek, sounding a crunch of facial bones and a crack from a twisted neck. Tyric spun, expecting another attacker, but none remained willing to pounce. The last two stood silent – caught in the tree's magic. Motes floated before their eyes that would hold them until they starved unless Tyric woke them. Tyric tossed the sword aside and wrenched his ax from the wizard. He searched the body but other than a few coins that he discarded to the ground, he found a ring of lightning bolts clutching a red ruby. He dropped the ring in his pouch and returned to the tree.

THWOQUE!

The night wore on and Tyric felled the tree. He methodically cleaned the limbs off and chained the trunk to the oxen. Pale motes of light continued fluttering up from the tree stump like new moths chasing starlight. He trimmed the larger branches and tied those to the main trunk with more chains.

Tyric dug in his pouch to look again at the ring he took from the dead wizard in the light from the tree, "Erolok might know why the Rubied Assassins seek my death in the wood." He tugged on the rope slipped through the oxen's nose rings and they lurched forward until the chains ground taught. The oxen leaned their shoulders into the yoke and pulled the timber into the dark forest. Loose ends of the chains rang hollow like old sleigh bells.

The two men remained unmoving and staring at the fiery stump – their faces slack and unthinking. They would nourish the tree's eventual re-growth unless their dead comrades found a way to wake them.

Chapter II: Enkarian Elf Castle

The fragrant smell of the burlap sack thrust through his wide leather belt wafted to Tyric's nose as he walked through the gates of the castle. The silvery rock of the castle stood strong and pristine as if no time had gnawed at its corners. However, it was an old castle built centuries before the nearly forgotten Great War a thousand years ago. Some suggested the castle stood here another thousand years before the War. Remarkable in that the castle remained one of the few outposts that withstood the attacks of the Shadow Wizard's armies – left a single rock upon a tall rock upon the mountain surrounded by scorched ruin. Its glittery gold spires atop the silvery white stone a reminder to the Shadow Wizard during the whole war that some could stand opposed to him. Then eventually the world repaired itself and forgot the devastation. The pristine woods returned in lush greens and browns. Speckled mountain flowers wafted fresh with morning dew as they hugged against the castle like a child against their father's sturdy legs.

"I'm here to see the King. He has armor that needs repair before the festival."

The slim elven guard looked over Tyric's sturdy frame, his thick arms, his bristly brows and black hair that brushed his shoulders. Not the thin trimmed blond hair of the castle guards nor any of the elves in the

Enkarian Forests. The wizard forge tattoos blazed along his forearms spoke as much his purpose as any statement or writ of letters might. "You have no weapons?"

"No."

The guard looked him over carefully, "Proceed." The guard pushed his hand against an ornately carved oaken door shod with silvery steel hammer-work hinges and latches and said, "Take this hall until you get to the end. Turn left. Ask for the Ward of the King's Arms."

Tyric stepped over the threshold from the morning light of the courtyard and into the darkness of the castle interior. The coolness of the stone brushed the air about him. Tyric's boots stopped banging hollowly on the corridor stone when he crossed onto ornate woven rugs laid down the hallway. The carpets absorbed not only the sound of his boots but any echoing noise from his chain mail and creaking belts. A lone candle burned in a wall sconce ahead where the corridor ended and went right and left. He stepped from the corridor into the intersection.

"Oh my goodness!"

"Sorry –" Tyric looked over the beautiful human woman wearing an ornate noble dress. Flowery blue like the mid-day sky stitched through with swirling patterns of green like the bright wood. The green of her dress and the dew-drop like pendant that quivered upon her breast sparkled and matched her emerald eyes. Her hair spun up against her head, secured with green headed pins leaving her neck bare. "I did not see you coming so fast."

She appraised his height, her eyes sweeping across his shoulders and back to his face, "I usually don't stroll. Nice to see another human here – we are in the minority."

"I won't be here long."

"Is that so?" her eyes scanned him; "You do not seem like a noble, you have working lines in your muscle. Yet your armor is more finely made than nearly all but a king's is. Not gaudy but sturdy, purposeful, and functional."

"I am a blacksmith."

"You do excellent work."

"How can one dressed as you are for a dance know what makes good armor?"

She smiled, "When one must choose who to wed, you become artful at identifying truth from fiction."

Tyric bowed, "You have caught me out of my element. I only came to the castle to retrieve the King's armor. He needs a few repairs before the next festival."

"Did he gain weight?"

"I wondered that too. But I suspect it will be mostly polishing and taking out a dent from when he fell off the battlement."

She put her hand to her mouth, "The King fell off the battlement?"

"That's the rumor, probably some stairs after a big drink, but you never know. A ding and some scrapes, and so I am here. I'm looking for the Ward."

"The Ward also acts as the castle Master of the Guard so he's often with the King. It's this way ahead." She pointed along to Tyric's left.

Tyric waved his calloused hand to the side and dropped his head, "I insist, after you."

She laughed, "Thank you, sir ...?" He ignored her question. She turned, her dress brushing along the carpet making more sound than his heavy work clothes and armor did, "I see wizard runes on your arms. You are more than just a blacksmith."

"Perhaps," a light smile came to his lips. "Or perhaps I find it safer to know you are in front of me rather than behind."

"You think I might attack you?" She stopped and turned to face him. "I am quite dangerous in this dress —"

"You only need to twirl and it will saw through the rock and my armor in a wink?"

"Yes. That's what it does. So you be careful," she turned her chin and continued ahead.

"That's why I wanted you in front. You seem too capable in that dress. Then, you also will catch any darting eyes when we step into whatever chamber is ahead."

"Darts or looks?"

"I never know what to expect in here. I dislike politics and that is all that goes on the closer to the throne room one gets. I enjoy the simpleness of being in the woods and the forge."

"Do you ever keep any company? In the woods?"

"None lately. But I can make exceptions."

"I thought I might ask your name. But now I think I shall not."

"It is Tyric. But I doubt you'll have time to use it

much except to explain to your friends who chased you through the corridor."

"They will only ask what new puppy I lured through the maze."

"And I will only have a story of a teasing emerald-eyed woman to make my friends marvel."

"Anika."

"Nice meeting you, Anika."

"I'd curtsy but we are already here."

Anika continued into the throne room without a break in her step as if she dwelt here every day and it was as easy as he went from his forge to his house. Tyric stopped at the edge of the doorway. Not out of awe of the glistening carvings in bright woods and stone and metals of every description, but appraising the layout of the entries and exits. This passage entered into the side of the hall. The main entrance was to his left out double doors many yards wide and high that sprawled open to the daylight of the inner courtyard. Thick columns flanked the entrance in an array where Tyric saw sufficient cover for both attackers and defenders. Another corridor continued across the room from the one he stood in. Behind the throne, a corridor passed between interior points of the castle, most likely the private quarters. Columns lined that corridor and an arch hung down giving the back wall behind the throne the look of a gallery. Tyric noted guards stationed in that gallery as well as along other points in the cavernous chamber.

The throne squatted at the top of a many tiered dais like lifting their King to the sky. The Enkarian King sat in working robes upon his throne, boredom painted across his countenance and shoulders as he worked through signing documents on a temporary desk. Groups of people loitered near him while others lined themselves along the great carpet that lolled like an old tired tongue out the open courtyard doors.

"This way," waved Anika.

Tyric finally followed her. His anxiety grew with the lofty ceiling and the wide space. While the pillars looked like the trunks of trees holding the roof high above as the sky it was not the same. Not the same as being out in the living world.

"Ward Gorlain!" Anika said as she came to the carpet.

The Master of the Guard looked up from his discussion with several nobles and smiled, "Yes, Anika?"

"This man Tyric is here to see about the King's armor."

"He is, is he?" Gorlain licked his aged lips, thin and white. "Have a stand over there Tyric. We'll keep you in order here."

Anika laughed and made a small wave at Tyric as she continued across the carpet and through the far passage. He watched her disappear around a bend in the corridor. He thought that was nice. Now for the waiting.

Tyric stood a while. First on one foot then on the other foot. He leaned against the column, noticing how others had leaned such and wore the wood wrapped stone over the centuries. A bad sign. He decided to stroll around and look at the carvings and metal work. Much of the work revealed delicate intricacies. Master artisans. He estimated the time to do this work, multiplying it over the number of columns and walls and ceiling. Eventually he wondered if he should start work on less ornate corners of the columns to dress them up more with new details since it seemed like he might still have time waiting yet. Tyric watched the King sign papers amid mumbled tones discussed between people waiting and those getting their business taken care of.

    The shadows along the carpet changed and Tyric glanced over and saw six men in leather armor walk from the bright light outside into the hall. Tyric saw how the metal buttons and buckles along with their empty scabbards showed abusive wear. He felt hopeful they might need his blacksmith shop before they left the castle. Their armor revealed the marks of heavy use and they walked with the strides of men comfortable with their skills in any environment.

    He noticed a chain about the neck of the leader when the man's eyes swept over everyone in the hall, apprising Tyric in the motion. Tyric saw that a ring dangled from the chain, brushed deeper into the man's tunic with a deft movement. The ring flashed a speck of red wrapped with an arc of lightning bolts.

    The guard asked, "Gentlemen, what business today?"

    The man with a chain said, "We intend to see the King about a fence on our property." He unrolled a large map of the area, parchment backed with thick leather and run through with heavy metal stays so it remained open. Tyric noted how it seemed too heavy for what the map construction suggested.

King Ek looked up from his papers and the business desk placed before the throne, "What is it these men want, Gorlain?"

"Sire, they have a dispute over a fence in the forest."

The King waved his hand. "We don't split the forest like farmer plots. We are the Enkarian Elves. We share our forest among ourselves. Not with ... men."

Gorlain said in quiet tones, "You will have to leave. The King has made his decision."

"But surely there is something that can be done?"

The King shouted, "Anika? Where is Anika?"

"Here, Sire," she bustled up the steps closer to the King.

"Bring me my wine, would you?"

"Sire, I see it is already being brought," Anika looked at a man dressed in the cook's clothes, somehow grubby and ill fitting. She looked at the man's face and saw he had the same appearance about him as the six men asking about the fence. She hurried down the steps to meet the cook before he came into sight of the King.

She whispered to him, "Who are you? A cook doesn't bring the wine out." She did not add that cooks remain hidden in the kitchen nor what Elven King would have a human cooking for him?

Tyric could see her trying to wrest the goblet from the resisting cook. Few others stood near vantage points to see them. She pulled at the cup and it spilled.

Anika said, "Sorry, Sire. Your wine has spilled. I will fetch it anew." Strange vapors arose from the spilled wine and dispersed. The cook stared at Anika as if he would kill her. He snatched at her neck and yanked away her necklace. Anika whirled and kicked her foot into the cook's chest and he flipped back, losing his hold on the chain. The bauble fell to the stones and it too released a strange vapor. Tyric wondered what this was.

The men with the dispute about the fence pushed anyone near them away as two of them ripped at the map. Enough slim daggers and flat swords fell out of the rents to arm the whole group. Four of them engaged the surprised guards and killed them while two others sprinted to the great doors and swung them shut with a bang and locked them solid with the cross-beam. Half of the people in the room managed to escape before two of the killers sprinted for the side corridors and the rear gallery to close and bar those doors tight. They herded everyone away from the exits and killed them. They came for Tyric.

"You will not escape," King Ek said, tidying his papers and putting down his quill. His assistant meticulously corked the inkwell and moved the papers over to the stack of others, his fingers shaking. The King's writing repeated one line, "Good King Ek is a very happy King." Occasionally he wrote "Good King Ek is very busy looking" or even "Good King Ek has seen a glorious sunrise today" even though it rained.

The leader of the men said, "But the prize is already here."

Tyric scooped up a short sword and spear from the

dead guard nearest him. He ripped the standard off the guard's ornate spear. Tyric knew the work of these weapons since he had forged the sword and repaired the old ceremonial spear. They would be serviceable.

"Why not run?" asked the leader of the group as they tightened near the steps to the throne. "You know who we are?"

Tyric paused, "I've already killed your friends. Do you fight any better?"

"What do you mean?"

Tyric tossed the ruby ring at them. It bounded up the steps before it stopped and lay still. "That ring looks just like yours."

"Where did you get that?"

"I took from a wizard that tried to murder me in the woods." Tyric waved the spear at the attackers, "I see no wizards among you."

King Ek's mouth draped open, "So you were marked? Too?"

The hard thump of rams came through the doors blocking the side tunnel from which Tyric entered.

Tyric said, "Sire, I don't know of any marks, but the friends of these men are dead."

"You are bottled off here," Anika said to the men as she came near the King.

Gorlain warned, "All we have to do is keep you talking and the whole guard will be here for you." His booming voice was punctuated by another strike of the ram against the heavy doors. Doors designed to keep attackers, not saviors, out of the great hall.

Four of the attackers rushed Tyric. Killing Gorlain

as they moved toward him. Another cut down the King's assistant that they had dragged off the dais.

The leader pulled his sleeves back revealing armbands of wizardry. Purple lightning rose over their heads and slammed down at Tyric, jerking like fingers.

Tyric's sword pierced the first attacker that struck Tyric's armor with his sword. Tyric stuck the spear through the chest of the nearest attacker wedging it in the man's rib cage. He pulled his arm back and thrust to the side with the short sword. The third attacker blocked his sword but Tyric's spear found the leg of the fourth attacker.

The electric fingers halted away from Tyric. Drained of their power. Anika saw a light blue effervescence emanate from Tyric and the magic soak into his glow.

Tyric knew the wizard had little chance against him. His gemstone protected him from such magic. He dragged the man with the spear pierced through his leg and both sides of his boiled leather armor. Tyric spun, lifting his prisoner in an arc that he released at the wizard. Tyric blocked the sword strike from the third attacker and shoved the sword under the gap in the man's armor. He felt the binding straps slice the seam of light chain-mail and leather split at the stitching. His sword dove into the man's flesh. The attacker fell to the floor dying.

Tyric came at the attacker that regained his feet with the spear still through his leg. Tyric observed the bulge through the muscle and guessed the spear rested against the man's bone as it pinned through him.

The wizard snarled and flung magic at Anika that

tumbled her backward behind the throne, unconscious.

Tyric grabbed the end of the spear and twisted it roughly. The man screamed and dropped his weapon. He fell to the floor trying to steady the spear. Tyric kept walking, pivoting the man about on the floor. He came at the wizard, now on his feet. The wizard burst lightning from his arms at Tyric. The energy approached Tyric but sucked into that same faint blue field that emanated from his body.

The wizard backed away. He cast another spell throwing fire streamers at Tyric. The fire either was absorbed or bypassed him to singe the screaming man Tyric dragged at the end of his spear. Tyric came at the wizard and spun his sword across, hacking the wizard's arms off at their elbows. When the wizard retreated, his back hit against a column, Tyric shoved the point of his short sword through the man's neck just above his collar with such force that the weapon wedged into the wood and pinned the body there.

He turned around and the man with the spear through him had hacked open his leg with a weapon he took from the floor and dragged himself away. He chewed something between his teeth and swallowed. Tyric came at the man with his sword and watched as the healing bar did its work. The attacker rolled aside and took up another sword. Tyric blocked the attacker's sword with the butt end of his spear and whipped the sharp blade across. The greater reach of his weapon arced over the sword and thrust through the chest of the attacker.

The rams punched at additional doors but all the beams held. Their booms echoed through the otherwise silent hall.

The King stood from his throne and walked toward Tyric, picking up Tyric's ruby ring and pulling the one from the slack necklace of the wizard pinned to the column. "You have two rings now – you are double marked." He pressed the rings into Tyric's hand. "I am glad you were here. My guards still bang at the doors." He shuffled across the steps and knelt beside Anika. Tyric straightened her leg and arm that had fallen under her. The King said, "The wizard seems to have put her to sleep." He looked up at Tyric. "You could kiss her and possibly awaken her."

Tyric's eyes flicked to her face, "Like the children's tales?"

"Could be. A good experiment to try? Like checking if the forge fire is hot." The King stood, his legs popping and cracking, "If she woke up and disapproved, you might wish for something as chill as a flaming forge fire." He laughed. "I recognize the magic. She will be fine. I have something to tell you."

"Tell me? About your armor?"

"Armor that I dented last year falling down the steps?" he smiled. "An old elf and his problems. No. The Rubied Assassin rings. They are an old guild. Mostly hidden and few know of them – until it's too late. They leave that ring after they kill someone. Only a few can afford to employ their expensive services."

Tyric said, "They tracked me into the forest and tried to kill me. What do assassins want with a blacksmith?"

"You are more than a blacksmith Tyric. Those

THE BLUE CRYSTAL

runes on your arms show you are progressing far in deep smith-work. You can toil with wizards and make weapons of power. Not a mere blacksmith that shoes horses."

"But I do shoe horses."

"You also have your own ring with a gem, am I right?"

Tyric turned his hand over and the blue nugget stone, rough and dull, set deep in a steel ring that Tyric had made sturdy so he did not lose it, hung on his smallest finger. A coarse worker's ring lacking in apparent value, jewelry that none would admire.

"Yes. That gem. You have always had it?"

Tyric nodded. Rams knocked again at the doors to the great hall. Tyric knew they would work long and hard and might have an easier time with the stones around the door.

"I need you to find something for me. In Emperor's Keep is hidden a special egg – a dragon's egg."

"Those are ruins, sacked in the Great War after Aleron was killed. There is nothing left."

"You have been there?"

"Once. To see what this land had been, but there was nothing. Broken rubble, tall columns toppled over, and smaller blocks quarried from larger blocks. Twisted clumps of brambles overgrowing portions of the ruins."

"Dark caves with nothing but feral night creatures lurking to frighten the children, too, I suppose. I think you speak the truth that you have been there." The King reached his arthritic hands to him, "Give me your hand." The King put his hands over and under Tyric's and a flash of fire entered the steel ring. The metal glowed for a moment and faded. "Your ring, not your gem, will be able to find and open the door. You now have the key. Inside will be the Dragon's Egg. I want you to get the egg of that special dragon hatched. We will need that dragon in the coming war."

"War?"

"The evil returns. An old evil? A new evil with the old tools? The old magic? Who knows yet? The purple lightning used by that wizard against you – that is old magic. Someone taught that to him."

"Then how did my gem stop it?"

"Your gem is old too," the King patted his arm and stepped toward his throne, "Don't tell anyone of this mission or it will be much more difficult than it already is." He winked his watery eyes at Tyric. "Open the doors."

Tyric walked to the doors and lifted the barrier. The guards streamed in.

The King said, "Where were my guards? These men almost killed me! And they spoiled my papers." The King waved his arms around in alarm. "Anika? Anika, where is my wine?"

"Eh?" Anika sat up, her hand at her head, "I will fetch it, Sire."

"Thank you, Anika."

A brusque elf shaped unlike most elves pointed his gauntleted fist, "Halt, you!" The elf could pass nearly as a human, a broad muscled thug that even when untroubled, his pinched nose and heavy brows made him look perpetually angry. Prince Elraf clanked across the floor in his heavy guardsman plate armor, a few pieces still unbuckled in his haste to assist the rescue. His fist remained pointed at Tyric. "Drop your weapons!"

"I killed the King's attackers," Tyric's eyes turned toward the King. The King had found some clean papers and gleefully marked them up. Laughing as he did so. The chatter of an insane King.

"We will see about that."

Chapter III: Dungeon

They clamped chains on Tyric's wrists and shuffled him down into the dark recesses of the castle's dungeon. The stink and the noise of centuries-old dampness whetted bones with their sunless chill.

Tyric stood behind the bars as the guards unlocked his manacles. Prince Elraf stood outside the bars and ran his eyes over the blacksmith. "You have the marks of an advanced blacksmith, but not all of them yet. This cell is cored with glagontyem, so you won't be able to get magic in or out, a cell that has held unspeakable monsters over the centuries. You will be nice and snug until we figure out what happened. Unfortunate that we cannot trust the words of our King. But we will investigate."

Tyric came close to the bars. Not sure how loud he should convey his words, "The attackers brought a ring of the Rubied Assassins." Somehow, he felt the glagontyem threaded around him like a bird cage against the magic of his ring that they let stay on his hand, probably because they understood the cell's magic.

Prince Elraf came close to the bars. Their breaths mingling between the black iron bars that separated them, "That will help your case if true. But how do I know you are not employed by them directly, or even indirectly?"

Tyric asked, "Do you think Gorlain killed those men? Do you think that woman Anika killed them?"

"What if you attacked the King and that group of men tried rescuing the King from *you*?"

"They brought enough weapons for all of them in that map of theirs. You saw I only held one, and used another. Both weapons from the guards. I would only need a few, not enough to equip a whole group."

The entrance gate banged shut and the guard rattled his keys in it.

"We will look. Perhaps we might find what you say." Prince Elraf turned and waved the guards along with him. Tyric could hear the layers of gates slam and jingle with keys in their locks. Each layer of portals increased the surety of remaining here, forgotten. Maybe his blacksmith teacher Erolok will look for him when the forge fades cold? The elf that raised him like his own son and taught him to work iron?

Chapter IV: Anika

The darkness stayed still and quiet. Tyric shook the lump of straw onto the box of a cot they gave him to sleep on. It at least smelled fresh like the field it came from but it made him feel like the hunting dogs bedding down. He had a blanket from a peg that hung on the wall. The elves never kept cruel prisons. Nevertheless, it was still prison. This would give him time to think through the words of the King.

Tyric remembered the way to Emperor's Keep. Marked on every map not as a fabled monument but as a place to shun, avoid treading there among the monsters. Give it wide space or the vestiges of the ancient forces that split it apart a thousand years ago might get the wanderer. He would have less fear of that, because he had been there once. He was more concerned with the King. The populace generally understood the unstable mind of the King. Madly working the day away scribbling nothing about nothing for weeks and months at a time. Occasionally the old mind seeped through whatever caused him his condition. Having a King with this ailment in a world in turmoil would be a risk to the elves but the relative peace in the world allowed the two princes and Gorlain to manage the kingdom's business needs.

A light scrape of a shoe on a cobble slightly higher than others in the passage scuffed outside his cell. Tyric clenched his fist and his gem ignited with sparkling bright bluish-white light, "Who is there?" The burst of light reached to the edges of his cage and then stopped. Everything beyond the bars remained in blackness. He released the magic of his gem.

"They must fear you to use glagontyem."

"Are you the woman from the throne room?"

Tyric heard the sound of thin sheaves of tin rotate, spin around, and a light shone from a small shrouded lamp smaller than a coffee cup. She set it on the floor near the barred door to his cell so that a tiny reflected beam danced across the lock face. "My name is Anika, if you've forgotten it already." She pulled metal implements that Tyric recognized as fine lock picks out of a rolled up sleeve and worked on the cell door lock.

"Those don't seem like the tools of a throne room girl. Where is your fancy dress? And chasing wine?"

"You think that I'm a trinket girl? Only suitable to fetch wine for the King? That dress is for the throne room, like armor for that special battle. I changed into a regular dress."

Tyric shook the straw off and hung his blanket on its peg. "I enjoyed talking with you. Is that why you have come here? To talk some more?"

Her motions with the lock paused for a heartbeat, then she continued gouging and working at the inner workings, "You'd like that, I'll bet. No. You saved the King."

"But you were asleep when it all happened."

"I believe you saved the King."

"Just from our short talk? You believe me?"

"Do you want to get released or do you want to stay here until they eventually remember you are locked up and might need to do something with you? The elves will rather leave you locked up than be forced to make a decision one way or the other."

"They will assume I am guilty if I run."

"Possibly. But there is evidence in the way you dispatched the attackers that says you protected the King from them, not that they defended the King against you. If they probe the evidence." A click and the lock freed itself. Anika put away her tools and pushed open the door, "Do you want to come with me or rot here and get executed for murdering important elves while threatening the King?" Tyric knew the elves would also seek her after enabling his escape.

"Lead the way," Tyric said, stepping forward into the passage.

"We will need to manage in the dark without the light," she lifted the little lamp. He saw her green eyes glitter in its small glow until she blew the light out. In the smell of the candle smoke, he realized how quickly his life had changed from an upstanding professional in the town to a criminal on the run. From light to dark in a breath.

Anika took them through a different route out of the prison than she used to get in. She picked several locks less complex than Tyric's cell that she could do by feel and they avoided new guards. She hurried Tyric along.

"I see the ground out that window, why are you going up more stairs?" Tyric whispered.

She said, "We're going to the roof."

They cut across the prison. None of the staircases went up more than a floor or two of the prison tower that rose as high as it plumbed the depths. The elves designed the prison to withstand internal riots or assaults from outside and so never gave straight passage from any two points easily.

They pushed through the final portal onto the roof stones. A gummy but not sticky roofing material pressed with stones coated the whole top of this tower.

Anika motioned to Tyric. She approached the furthest ledge from the door and reached out. Tyric saw a thin cable tied tight to the tower with a grapnel hooked behind it. Anika leaned through the battlement gripping the rope tightly. In the sound of a swooping bird, she was gone along the cable. She disappeared along the spider silk thin rope at an angle into the darkness high enough it cleared the outer wall. While he could see fairly well in the dark, he found he could hardly see her. Her dark clothes faded into a shadowy almost shifting fog that coiled around her. His arms and body shown almost bright white in contrast to her. What magic was she using? Who was this girl?

Tyric leaned over, gripped the cable, and slide along it. His hands, rough from the forge, still heated and burned. He twisted his legs into the rope to reduce the load on his hands. He dared not look down at the empty void between him and courtyard stones. Then he came to the edge of the castle wall. He stepped onto the stones. His hands throbbing. Anika materialized out of the shadows.

"I should have given you these." She handed him a

pair of gloves with thick leather palms. He tried forcing his hands into the gloves but the gloves would not give to his big hands.

"My hands are too big from working the forge fires."

"Then use what you can. We go down this rope from here." She spun on her hand hold and dipped out of sight over the wall. Tyric looked over the edge at the chilling chasm that dropped off the edge of the castle mountain. He wedged the gloves on as much as he could and followed Anika down the second rope.

They slid below the trees and then came to the ground. Anika shimmered out of the darkness, releasing whatever magic she had used. He saw she wore a tight fitting black suit with leather armor riveted in places but with fire blackened steel so nothing glinted. "Any opinion on what town we should consider hiding in for a few years?"

"I don't know about a few years, but I have a project to finish. I need my weapons and my other armor from my home."

"We will have to hurry. Are we close? If it's on the other side of the castle we'll have to forget it."

"No. This way." Tyric followed a rising ridge that snaked across this part of the forest like one of the little toes of the mountain range. The sky lightened by the time they came to his small cabin. They hung in the shadows fearing guards might watch his house if they discovered his escape. They observed the house for some time before Tyric crept toward the rear door. Anika held back by a large hickory, the shaggy bark like rough fur up and down the timber. Anika lost sight of

Tyric when he went inside.

Tyric listened for any sound and looked around. Nothing had been disturbed since the day before. He found his armor and quickly got into it. He didn't worry about buckling and buttoning it down but it would be easier to carry if worn. He took his ax off the wall above the fireplace. He filled his large leather backpack with anything he could think of needing. A jaunt of salt pork, small cooking pots, forks, and spoons. He could live rougher but it might be nice to have a bit more equipment for Anika. He put his heavy boots on and worried about lacing them later. His cloak and shield were the last he clutched as he walked out the door and back to Anika. They faded into the brush before talking.

She asked him, "Are you sure you need all that?"

"Did I ask you to carry some of it?"

"No. But that's a big sack to carry."

Tyric held a branch from slapping at her, "We are going for an extended trip, right? We need provisions."

Anika paused, "Where are we going?"

"Emperor's Keep."

She shook her head, "No. Not there."

"Why not?"

"What's there? No one ever returns."

"Some do."

"None I've ever heard of." She cleared the throw of the branch and Tyric let it swish free.

Tyric tightened his boots, "I've been there once."

"How did you survive?"

"I didn't stay the night nor go into too many dark holes," he stood. "This time I will."

"You think I want to? We can hide out in Ket, Tadur, or Dekvor. Alternatively, each of them, stay in any one of them for years and then move. Your smith-work skills will mean you won't starve in any place. Your skills are in high demand."

"And what do your skills add up to?" They walked. Tyric knew the general direction they needed to travel.

"I'm just a girl that gets wine for the King."

"Maybe I should be King?"

"If you were King," Anika tramped passed Tyric. "You'd still need to get your own wine."

Chapter V: South to Ruins

Prince Elraf knelt by the stream and lifted water to his lips. The cold water tasted good and clear. He needed to think about where Tyric might be going. His team had found the ropes and the escape path. That human Anika appeared to have released Tyric. The Prince brought twenty of the guard with him on this chase, and they sought revenge. His brother gave him a wizard apprentice to aid them in finding Tyric.

"Sir, the wizard found their path again. They stopped at the stream and veered away from the stream after the tall pine. They are going south."

Prince Elraf stood and shook the water from his hand, "What is their destination?" He knew most of the known world was south of here. They could be going anywhere.

The air was hot and humid. "I need to clean up."

"You look fine and I cannot smell you yet." Tyric said.

"Says the one who needs a good scrubbing."

"I have worked long and hard on this particular odor. I think it is a popular one."

"You are mistaken." Anika unwound her hair letting it down while she unbuttoned her dress and slipped out of it. She dove into the frigid water with soap cream on her hand and quickly scrubbed herself.

She came out of the water and wrapped a blanket about herself. "You can use some of my soap." Anika watched Tyric remove his armor and his shirt. His knobby blacksmith body drew her eyes with more desire than she expected, or wanted. "Catch." she tossed her soap to Tyric.

He caught the soap, turned, removed his trousers, and stepped into the water. The stream moved more swiftly than it appeared from the surface. He first scrubbed away the scaly blood left over from his battle saving the King and then the rest of himself. He strode out of the stream squeezing the water from his mane and beard and Anika sat on a large flat rock dressed in a fresh traveling dress with trousers.

"Where did you get the extra clothes?"

"Feminine wiles. My pack is larger than it looks." Her eyes brushed up and down his wet body. She covered her smiling mouth with her hand, "Good to see you got the battle washed off finally."

"Yes." Tyric dressed. "We need to keep moving." He noticed her appraising gaze when he slipped over his shirt before shifting into his armor.

"I agree. I'm just waiting for you."

"The road will be hard, are you sure you don't want to go somewhere else? The road is not a place for a pretty girl."

"I can handle myself on the road." She stood, "What did the King tell you?"

"He told me to go south. Find my fame and fortune."

"Not rot away in the city of elves?"

"I see you understand." Tyric slung his equipment over his shoulder and she followed him south.

The forest opened into small farm plots that wrapped around gigantic trees. The trees were so tall and old and the spaces between them so wide that the sunlight could get to the ground where the elves farmed.

Anika knelt beside a small bush, "What is your name?" She scratched the ear of a half-grown white goat that chewed leaves off the side of it.

"We don't need to make friends with the goats. Nor dally since we will have followers."

Anika said, "We are going to need provisions in addition to the ones you brought."

"I have no coin."

"But I have a few." Anika walked the path through the field. The goat decided she was good to follow, and so it bleated behind her as they crossed toward the sod hut built tight against one of the tree trunks. Tyric saw the hut was actually a little barn for the goats. He looked around and wondered where the farmer lived.

"Over here." Anika said, knocking at the tree trunk.

Presently a thin crack split around the shape of a door in the side of the tree and it opened up. An old elf pushed open the door and leaned on it as he shuffled out. Tyric saw the deep carving that curled into faint lighting of the interior rooms cut inside the tree. A spiral staircase coiled around the inside of the tree and up beyond where he could see.

"Can I help you?" the old elf asked, raising his

eyebrow to Tyric and then looked over Anika.

The goat tipped its head, its floppy ears slapping against its cheeks as it looked from one to the other.

"You're Ejryl the goat farmer, aren't you?"

"That I am."

"I've had your cheese at court. Fantastic stuff. What can you spare for a couple of travelers?"

"The King's chef bought most of my stock, the rest I have is too new and not good yet. But I might have a few wedges still." His eyes twinkled and he said, "I know you," he pointed at Anika, "You're from the court. I saw you helping the King with his wine or something." He walked into his tree and disappeared. Soon he returned with several wedges. "Here, I found a few wedges the chef missed." Anika gave him a few coins and took the cheese from him.

"That's too much. I don't have change for that."

"I wasn't looking for change."

"Then wait here —" He reappeared with a paper wrapped package tied with coarse string and a loaf of crusty bread. "Take these. That package is dried goat meat. It will travel well as long as you keep it dry."

Anika took the items and bowed her head, "Thank you, Ejryl."

They continued through the forest. Tyric said, "That will keep us from eating squirrels."

"That's what I thought you might try to feed us."

"They are plentiful in the forest and easy to catch."

* * *

"Ejryl it is?"

"Yes, Sir," the elf bowed more than most might, even when knowing it was the King's son.

"When did they come through here?"

"Which they? I have many customers for my wares."

Rulvog, an elf with scars of an old sword wound crossing his face, said, "Prince Elraf has asked you a simple question. Where are they? The man and the woman?"

"The man and the woman came through earlier this morning."

Prince Elraf said, "They endangered the King. They have eluded the castle watch. They escaped from the dungeon."

"That seems serious," Ejryl nodded.

"That is why the King's son is personally tracking them," said Rulvog. He grabbed the old elf by the arm and held him. "Tell us more details of how you helped them."

"I only helped them as far as they paid for my wares. Simple cheese. They said they went south"

"What else did they tell you?" Rulvog drew his dagger and held its point against the older elf's chest.

"That is all I know. They went south and I sold them cheese. You must believe me."

Rulvog grabbed the elf's shaggy gray hair, dragging the knife across his skin threatening an easy dip through his throat.

"Enough, Rulvog." Prince Elraf waved his hand.

"But Sir –"

"No. We will be civil. Ejryl is elderly, he has shared what information he has, and we should leave him."

"How do we know he is not lying or withholding information? We must extract it from him," Rulvog squeezed his fist.

"We will not. Ejryl has freely shared information with us."

Ejryl agreed, "Yes. All that I know."

Prince Elraf said, "And we can see their path went South before and it looks to continue south." He flicked his gauntleted hand, calling back his trackers. "We will go now. Thank you for your time Ejryl."

"– But surely, Sir ..."

Prince Elraf bowed, "Come Rulvog." Prince Elraf strode along the path their quarry had taken south. Rulvog glared at the elderly elf and released his arm. He tromped after Prince Elraf with the others.

Chapter VI: The Dogs

"Something smells bad." Tyric smelled the air again.

Anika turned her head about the darkening gloom as they walked along the path, and sniffed, "I don't smell anything but the wood."

"It's quiet, too. I do not hear any crickets." Tyric tugged at the straps that tied his ax to the armor plate across his chest. The weapon fell comfortably into his fists.

"The crickets likely quieted because of us. You have a heavy tread."

"It's this armor and my thick legs." His alertness warned of something unnatural.

Anika splayed one hand to quiet Tyric and drew a dagger from her belt with the other.

Tyric moved so his back faced a thick oak opposite of where his uneasiness came from. He scanned the moving branches fluttering in the light breeze. He wished for no wind but he knew if something stirred in the wood, it would do more than this breeze. Anika stepped along the path. Tyric saw how she moved with the caution and the grace of a hunting cat – reeking of the exactness that came from consistent heavy training. Tyric scanned the falling darkness. Night came quick and abrupt. Anika motioned with her hand again, pointing to his right, the far side of him from where she stood. He looked and saw nothing. The shadows twisted in lurid fantasies that he blinked back. Then he did smell something. Putrid and hot like a damp breath filled with harrowing death that made his nerves urge flight. He saw an eye. Black and anger-filled that swiveled from Anika to him, a spiky furred snout that eased slowly between leaves in the underbrush. Tyric cast his ears wide and heard a slow pant behind them. Anika put a third finger out and twisted her hand to reveal another adversary further ahead along the path. Tyric held up four fingers when he heard another approach from the other side of the tree behind him. With Anika's attention, he motioned for her to draw back. They needed to be closer for the coming attack.

Anika stood beside the tree with him. A hooting growl deeper in the forest echoed through the wood and vibrated their chests. Tyric knew the creatures came soon – savage teeth and as tall as he at their shoulders. Tyric put his hand to Anika's shoulder and tugged her up, directing her to climb the tree. She shook her head and pulled another dagger from a hidden sheath among her clothes. Her skirt fell away revealing leather leggings that gave her more movement. He would have to ask her about this. If they survived these massive mountain dogs.

The first dog rushed through the underbrush. Its teeth filled the air sparkling like stars in the growing gloom. Tyric's ax met against the skull splitting it from snout to eye. The bristly stiff fur ground against his knuckles like unpolished chain mail. The fur was already wet but the powerful dog fell like jelly against him. Tyric barely bent aside as the bulk of the monster struck the tree and fell into a wall of flesh. Anika's daggers flashed away in the gloom. Tyric realized that she had slit its throat along with his strike splitting its skull. Who was this woman?

A pair of mountain dogs circled and attacked from both flanks. Tyric brought his ax around and up, slicing through the first dog's throat and then bashing the second through the teeth accelerated by his thick forge-strong shoulder. Anika killed one of the mountain dogs but the second reached for her thigh. Tyric leaped at the monster and checked its head with his back plate and his own bulk that bent the dog's head away. He reached a hand to the monster and gripped a fist-full of fur. He tugged himself along the dog and brought his ax around to strike down like a hammer on an anvil. The spine of the dog fractured before its edge and the rear half of the monster flopped down broken to the dirt. Its wide snout sought him and gave nothing but a grunt at the pain. It reached for him but flailed as Anika's twin daggers struck into it.

Then an angry half dozen monsters pressed at them fueled with the stench of their dead comrades. Tyric waded into them holding his ax in both hands and swinging in a ferocious attack that dropped three of the dogs by clipping through their beam-like legs and tearing through their rib cages. Behind his movement, Anika followed him and finished any of the dogs that needed threat adjustments.

The first mountain dogs were shaggy and gray. Now two more came at them nearing jet black in color with fiery red eyes that glowed unnaturally from the darkness hanging around them now. Hulking dead bodies piled like hills to their right and left making their stand treacherous. The two massive dogs circled, growling and barring their teeth.

"They will attack soon," Anika said to Tyric.

"As long as they do not await reinforcements."

"They might."

"Then I cannot give them a chance."

"– No!"

Tyric halted his attack and reset his stance, "What then?"

"Choose your first target carefully, and I will assist."

Tyric shrugged his shoulder and spun his ax between his fingers. He charged the nearest mountain dog only to find it fade back while the second animal lunged toward him. Tyric turned on his heel and sliced his ax at the second mountain dog. It bowed its head down under the ax blade as he brought it across, flattening its ears so even the hairs tufting off their tips avoided the dangerous edge. The dog sprang up under the swing and clamped down on Tyric's armor-covered arm. While the strong bite could not crush his well-made armor, its neck flexed and flipped him into the air. The strap tethered the ax to his wrist or he would have lost his weapon into the underbrush. His body struck a tree and he fell into a roll across sharp brambles that held him fast. The brambles bowed in every direction as he struggled to regain his footing. The second mountain dog neared with a low guttural growl and stepped uncaring through the brambles. Tyric fought to pull himself up. Then rolled his body over the springy wood away from the searching bites. Tyric gripped his ax and swung it through the brambles until he cut himself free. He stood amid the ripping thorns as if protected from a moat but the mountain dogs came at him heedless of their claws. As the teeth of the dogs reached for him, he found himself forced to use his arms and body to protect his face from the ripping jagged thorns that closed around him in the darkness. Where was Anika?

The dogs snapped at him and nearly tore his arms off when they clamped down upon him. He flexed his arms and wrapped himself tight. Gritting his teeth, he curled his arms and ground one arm free of a dog. His ax arm still held tight between jaws. Tyric yanked at the dagger on his belt and thrust the sharp point through the side of the dog's head. The puncture wound only seemed to increase the clamp force exerted by the growling dog. Tyric levered the end of the dagger up like twisting a rusted, unforgiving bolt with a wrench. He felt his dagger flex under his grip but also the dog's head moved and opened. He twisted the blade along its axis and the lever turned into its cutting edge. He strained and the blade gouged deeper into the skull.

The first dog bit across his torso, he felt his ribs flexing below his protective armor. His mind flashed along the strength ribs he built into the armor to absorb such force and wondered if the armor could hold. The dog yanked at him and tore his arm out of the first dog's bite. He lost hold of his dagger and the dog worried him, bashing his shoulders against a thick coiled section of the brambles. He felt helpless and reached for his ax but the weapon flailed at the end of the tether just out of his reach.

He saw flashing steel whir through the darkness and puncture one of the red eyes of the beast that held him. Then a second blade tumbled and sunk through the dog's ear canal. The biting grip about his torso shuddered and fell away. Tyric picked himself up and raced at the remaining dog, his fingers yanking at the tether and running along the grip of the ax. He stabbed at the dog with the sharp tip and then swung the blade at it. The dog snapped its black teeth, its red eyes piercing the night like lances, angry points of light that Tyric used to aim his attack. The dog lunged at him and he dropped his foot to pull back and allow the dog near. Then he sprung off his foot, swung the ax around, and down as if mashing the first billet of hot steel. The blade bit into the skull to the shaft. He wrenched it free and raised his fist for a second strike but the dog toppled to the leaf covered soil.

"You are good with that ax."

"I chop a lot of wood and bash out a few weapons and armor for the elves."

"And that armor of yours, not like any I've seen."

"It's not. I designed extra hoop strength into it. Glad I did. Conventional armor and I would have been crushed."

The two black dogs glowed a reddish purple phosphor.

"What's going on?"

"No idea," Tyric stepped away from the nearest of dog. The glow around the first dog faded but in the darkness it remained difficult to discern the dog's features. Tyric's eyes adjusted.

Anika saw first, "shape shifting wizards! Wait –"

"Why didn't they change into wizards and attack with spells?"

"Those are not men or elves, they are korlak."

"Korlak? Maybe they were tied too tight to the magic of the form they took." Tyric prodded the nearest wizard with his ax. Tattered robes and bloody wounds crossed their tattooed bodies. The cleft skull cracked open like a broken egg shell. Runes tattooed along their arms and faces showed the deep magic. Tyric recognized a few symbols, ones that matched the marks along his arms and torso, and ones he knew to come eventually. "They have forged weapons of power. Why are such wizards following us?"

"The elves want us."

Tyric said, "No. The elves wouldn't use korlak to chase us. They'd use elven wizards; or rather are using elven wizards."

Anika retrieved her daggers, "Why are the korlak after you?"

"Why do you think they are after me? They might want you. Or we stumbled into their little patrol out here."

"I'd think they were on patrol. That seems like the clearest possibility."

"Yes. That might seem like a clear explanation." Tyric gathered his lost pack and the scattered equipment flung off his body during the fight. He thought he had everything. "Tell me why you are more than just a wine girl for the King."

"I also fetch other things for the court."

"You have more skills than many men I've seen."

She slid her daggers home, "No. I don't have any more skills than any girl that had to learn to survive on the streets. The wine girl job is just easier work."

Tyric looked through the tree limbs scratching at the sky. A glow of moonlight hinted along the horizon. "I don't feel like setting up camp – I won't be able to sleep for hours anyway. I want to push ahead and give us more space between the elves at our back and these wizards and any possible friends looking for them, or us. The moon will give us light ahead."

Anika peered through the gray gloom and nodded, "Lead the way."

* * *

"Sir, mountain dogs."

"Where? –" Prince Elraf's shoulders cocked up and his foot slid to his practiced stance, his hand dropping to the hilt of his weapon.

"No, Sir. They are dead. And two creatures I have never seen."

One of the older warriors asked, "How many years have you been scouting? To not recognize creatures in the wood?"

"This way." He diverted the group from the path and came to the mountain dogs scattered around the forest floor. Scavengers already feasted on the dog bodies but they stayed clear of the two smaller figures.

"Didn't your mother ever tell you about the stories

of the korlak hiding in the mountains to the east?" The warrior slapped the back of the younger scout and laughed.

Prince Elraf kicked the body over with his boot. "Korlak. With the marks of a wizard." He studied the bare arm and the side of the creature's face. The sun was high and hot. His mind flashed back to years ago, "Don't be too harsh with our scout. I've only seen three in my lifetime. My father captured several along the edge of the mountains. We thought they might be spying on us but none came after."

"These are deep in our lands."

Prince Elraf nodded. "They might be more important than the blacksmith and the girl. Wizards leading mountain dogs this far into our kingdom, undetected."

The older elf said, "Sir, I've been hearing reports of other beasts, too."

Prince Elraf said, "Yes. But easy stories of missing livestock or strange footprints among the orchards told by the uneducated and the fearful? By the drunk just from the tavern? Any reputable stories from the guard?"

"No, Sir."

Prince Elraf said, "Dump your bag out."

"Sir?"

"Dump your bag out and," Prince Elraf gripped the wrist of the nearest korlak and lifted the arm. He unhooked his throwing ax from his belt and chopped down against the shoulder joint. The sharp ax cut true and clean. He glanced at the side of the blade and saw the blacksmith they chased had made it. "Put that in the bag."

"It won't fit, Sir."

Prince Elraf turned his head, his eyes squinting in anger but he kept his voice level, "Then leave the claw out, it will wave to us as you run through the wood back to the fortress."

"Oh."

Prince Elraf gave the arm to the scout and then gripped one of the spikes on the korlak's head to hold it still and chopped through its thick neck. He handed the head to the scout. "That should be enough for my brother to use his magic and discern more than what we know. You can describe the rest of what we see here?"

"Yes," the young scout nodded.

"I would send another with you but from what I see here and the damage the blacksmith did, I will need as many as I can keep. Now go."

The scout saluted and ran north.

"Prince," Rulvog laughed, "I see the korlak's claw waving to us."

Chapter VII: Cave Pets

Tyric and Anika came to a clearing in the forest. A pale waving meadow with a swamp on the left and a rising bump to the right ringed with thicker underbrush that hungered for that open space. Tyric motioned to Anika to turn before they came to the brush. Anika halted, "The meadow will be easier and faster to travel along."

"So is the forest between the larger trees."

Anika held up her arms, "My arms are itchy from the scratching branches."

"As are my wounds from the brambles."

"You seem to be healing quickly."

"Fortunate, I guess." Tyric rubbed his face, "If wizards and dogs still chase us the meadow is bad."

Anika said, "We killed them."

"And how did I get so fortunate my traveling companion is so skilled, from living on the streets, as you say?"

"I learned a few things from the other women," Anika said.

"Thieves?"

"A few. I found an old neighbor who traveled with a circus troop and did knife throwing."

"That is a good trick."

"It's not a trick –"

"I know. It saved me back there. That dog almost bashed me against one of the oaks."

Anika stood with her hands on her hips, "You could trust me."

"Did I say I did not trust you? We've been running and hiding since you got me out of that dungeon. Why would I not trust you? It's not like I'm a prince heir to a kingdom that you want or anything. I'm just a working blacksmith."

"You are more than a blacksmith. You work with Erolok and you can make items of power."

"– You seek power?"

"No. The elves will need weapons."

"For what?"

Anika stopped and put her hand to Tyric's shoulder, "While I am in court I hear all the King hears –"

"So you're a spy?" Tyric's eyes searched her face.

"No. I hear stories of the Old War. The King searched for something because he fears the time is returning for a Second War. Korlak wizards – here – they fought the Old War –"

"So you think I want to return and help the elves?"

"Yes. The Enkarian Forest is your home. I think you have some secret that propels us toward danger –"

"– Hush!" Tyric freed his ax and spun the tether tighter over his wrist. The ground rumbled nearby. A bump of dirt split above the meadow like the air blow of a whale and then silence stilled across the forest. Tyric took a step forward, searching the forest to the sides and above them. He picked several more steps through the crunchy leaf bed between the roots of the tall oaks.

The ground erupted in front of them. Dirt, leaves, and small half-rotted sticks rained down. Two enormous worms opened port-hole mouths filled with rows of triangular shovel-shaped teeth. Their hides scintillated in the sunlight throwing rainbow hues in a sparkling array of color that shimmered and permeated the air in a mesmerizing glow.

"Tunnelers!" Tyric yelled, remembering a tale told in a tavern when he was a boy. He and Anika split away. The worms chased them, slamming into the ground, disappearing underneath, and then popping up somewhere else ahead of them. A third scintillating creature surged from the ground in a slightly different hue, coiling up from the exploding soil flashing its teeth and biting at them. The story told him they needed protection, "Stone!" The last of the tunnelers coiled around the nearest oak following the sound of Tyric's voice. He knew the only protection against the attacks of a tunneler would be massive stone slabs. Stone littered the forest, but only head and torso sized chunks, not continuous plates protecting them like islands. He sped toward the brush and the meadow, "The bump might be stone!" Anika turned away from the attacking tunneler and followed Tyric through the brush and into the open meadow.

The tunnelers rose out of their ground holes searching the lengthening distance to their prey. They struck like swamp cobras out of the brush and leaped into the meadow. Tyric flung himself aside as the brutes slammed into the ground, jostling each other.

They were gone again as quickly as they had appeared. The silence of the meadow ticked away with their heartbeats. The breeze swished the grass and buffeted across their ears as they stood on the slight mound. Straining their hearing to search for the rumbling that preceded an attack. They dared not move for fear the tunnelers would sense their actions against the ground.

Anika pointed to the little knob they stood on, mouthing, "Stone?"

Tyric shook his head.

An ominous slithering rippled under Anika's feet. Silver and violet scales of a tunneler burst from the ground as a dolphin shooting from the water to take a treat from its trainer's hand, but this animal wanted the whole hand, the arm, and everything from Anika. She balanced on the lip of the tunneler as it shot up into the air. She flipped back and landed on her feet but then sprawled out flat in a roll away from the monster. The tunneler twisted itself, gnashing angry teeth that growled through the space toward Anika.

Tyric lined up with the trunk of the tunneler and hewed his ax at the base as if felling a tree. He swung, but the tunneler struck into the ground where Anika had laid and it disappeared before his swing caught more than the tapering tip of its tail.

The earth eroded under Anika. The dust shook and she fell with the disappearing soil, "Help me!" Tyric only saw the last of her fingers disappear into the darkness followed by soil and the little white flowers that peppered the meadow.

A tunneler coiled out of the ground behind him and arced down seeking him. Tyric swung his ax at the monster with three strikes that each would have easily felled a stout oak. The tunneler rolled its tubular body away and then a second tunneler shot up out of the ground from the hole where Anika disappeared. He sliced at the monster with his ax, this time connecting with a long curved arc. The first tunneler batted him aside. Tyric tumbled across the dirt and grasses. The little white flowers poked at his eyes when he finally stopped rolling. He growled as he sprang from his hands and knees to his feet and charged the two tunnelers that dove for new holes in the ground. He leaped over open mounds and dark shafts. He jumped at the nearest tunneler with his ax before him like a double bladed lance. His weapon dug through the tunneler and burst through the opposite side. Tyric's ax head poked through the far side of the tunneler's tail while the rest of the weapon and his whole arm to his shoulder stuck in the cold worm. The tunneler flipped its tail trying to dislodge him but he stayed pinned as the length of the beast dove underground again. The monster would shear him off at the crease between the monster and the ground!

 Tyric's free hand reached for the sword at his waist. His fingers stretched for the pommel nut. Then they coiled around the grip. He pulled the weapon and hacked at the monster to free his other arm. His sword cut into the flesh of the tunneler but at a bad angle. The ground came close. He shoved the tip forward until the sword blade ground against his ax and the wall of the tunneler gave way. Tyric dropped to the ground and the monster's tail followed it into the ground. Tyric pushed himself to his feet and ran toward the hole where Anika disappeared.

"Drop me a rope," Anika whispered from the dark hole.

Tyric set his weapons down and uncoiled the rope from his belt, being careful to avoid moving his feet. He could not see her. He lowered the end of the rope into the hole until he feared he would be out of rope. He felt a tug on the rope as Anika wrapped her hand and wrist into it securely and said, "Pull."

Tyric gripped the rope and pulled her up, hand over hand. His ears remained alert for any noise from the tunnelers. Finally, he saw her hand and he reached down to grip her fingers. A scintillating worm cut across the hole, sucking Anika into its mouth as it twisted forward through the earth. Its sharp teeth slicing the cord from his connection to her. Tyric wrenched the sword and ax from the ground. He struck into the undulating shimmering monster as it moved beneath him, drawing nasty gashes as the creature disappeared.

The ground blew open behind Tyric in a burst of dust and roots. The nose of a second tunneler bumped him into the air. It surged forward snapping teeth and moaning. Tyric twisted in the air by swinging his weapons wide. The giant mouth lunged and closed. Tyric crashed his ax against the plate-like teeth and pushed himself away. The worm surged and bit at him. Tyric drove the sword into the muscular ring around the mouth and hung on as the worm bucked back. As he approached the zenith of the worm's arc, he twisted the handle of the sword. When the worm snapped itself back down the sword tore through its vicious mouth.

Tyric fell against the tunneler's body and then slipped to the ground. He could only think of Anika. *How much air does she have?*

The third tunneler burst out of the ground when it felt Tyric's feet strike across the meadow as he ran. He came to the first tunneler and saw only an empty hole. He swung down into the tunnel and raced along it. He pushed his mind through the magic of the ring on his finger and light cut into the darkness ahead as he ran. Tyric could have marveled at the tunnel construction and by the liquid that squeezed against the walls from the creature's wounds if he did not need to pursue Anika.

A tunneler burst through the side wall behind him, while another punched down from above. Tyric slid by the gap before it closed and sprinted ahead. The tunnel screwed into the ground and then rose toward the surface before twisting back around and –

"*Greedy worm wants both of us,*" Tyric spun in the tunnel and hefted his ax. He knew there was no escape from the teeth that would ring the whole tunnel.

The tunneler sped at him with snapping teeth. He bashed against the teeth with his ax and stabbed at the ring of muscle with his sword. He backed up and struck into the tunneler with his ax. His sword buried deep into the monster and it slunk back, yanking the sword from his hand.

How much air does Anika have? How long have I chased this thing? Will she be alive?

Tyric charged the worm. He leaped over the ring of teeth before they closed on him. The muscles of the tunneler's digestive tract worked at compressing him.

He pitched forward when the tunneler bumped and moved. Disoriented, he knew not if the worm went up or down, left or right, or just spiraled into the deep earth. He could only see in the flickering light from his ring the undulating pinkish curtains of muscle that ganged together to squeeze him further along. Like a ship lurching among roiling waves he struggled to stand. The space he braced his feet was too tight to swing his ax. He stabbed the blades against the worm, his shoulders and arms flexing, pushing and prodding the tough lining. His blade punctured the beast. He heaved repeatedly and the gash widened, pulling flesh back and providing more space. He turned and chopped into the opposite side of the worm. Then what seemed like the floor.

The worm slowed and it stopped. A shudder quivered through it. Tyric did not stop. He kept hacking until he sliced through it. His boot slipped and he fell to his hip through the opening at the bottom of the worm. One hand gripped at the slippery edge of cut flesh. He pulled himself up and looked through his incisions. He stood over another tunnel that went down into deep darkness.

He took a step and cut again until he freed a wheel-like wafer from the creature's body that slipped and disappeared down the shaft. It never made any noise as if it never hit the deep bottom of the shaft. Moist mud and intestines from the worm continued oozing into the opening.

Tyric pried at the interior of the tunneler. He wedged his ax head and levered more of the guts into the pit. He did not think and ponder if or how long before he might find Anika. His shoulders worked at gutting the monster. He hacked at it like jelly seeing internal organs unlike anything he had ever seen, but then he did not normally take earth worms apart either. He hoped the other tunnelers would leave him alone inside the body of one of their own.

He saw an opaque sack holding a human form. He worked fast to cut enough of the intestines that its weight would not pull Anika down the shaft. He gripped her ankle, yanked her from the stomach, and dropped her onto a stable portion of the worm. She did not move.

He touched her and found a pulse but she did not breathe. He cleared slime from her face and pushed on her chest to expel more goop from her nose and mouth. He used his hand on her cheeks to revive her. Her lids fluttered and she took a full draw of air. Her eyes went from the unfocused startle of awaking from a nightmare to awareness. She sat up. "I couldn't breathe!"

"I almost didn't get you out –" Tyric said. The ground around them rumbled. "We must move." Tyric gripped his ax, he took Anika about her waist and leaped over the hole into the front of the tunneler and pushed through until he squeezed them between the gaping mouth. He carefully stepped over the teeth and they ran farther along the tunnel.

A tunneler shot through the ground where they had stood then sank back bobbing in a sea of soil until it twisted around finding them. It carved into the soil back and forth filling everything with a mist of dirt and rock. It bent toward them and struck.

"Let me go." Anika pushed away from Tyric and ran along the tunnel ahead of him. Tyric stayed close. Another tunneler crossed the tunnel behind them.

Tyric said, "We need a tube to the surface –"

Anika stopped, "Shhh!"

Tyric froze with her, straining his ears for sounds and searching out vibrations through his boots.

Anika reached for Tyric and pulled herself tight against him. A tunneler burst from the ceiling and sped down where Anika had stood, burrowing deeper.

She tapped Tyric's shoulder and pointed behind them. A shaft of light from the world above burned into the dark tunnel. They ran for the tunnel following the light. Explosions of soil filled the air behind them with debris as the tunnelers cut across their escape route. Dust billowed first behind them then around them and then ahead of them shooting out of the tunnel to the surface in an angry cloud.

Tyric snatched Anika's hand and pulled her aside. Two of the tunnelers surged out with the cloud of dust snapping at it searching for the two humans. He pushed her back and gripped his ax with both hands. He coiled his body from his calves, his thighs, his back, his shoulders, and his arms and powered them forward to bring the ax down. The ax cut deep into the two tunnelers. Such a swing meant to squeeze thick bars of hot iron between his heaviest hammer and the sturdy black anvil pitched his body forward. He pushed with his toes, tucking his body into a forward roll that brought his ax around another complete swing and sliced through the second tunneler.

Tyric straightened his body and twisted about an axis that landed him on his feet and ready with his ax in the air over his shoulder. The tunnelers flopped on the ground, severed through except for a thin strip of skin and quivering muscle. The ground below them vibrated with the death throes of the tunneler's tails.

Tyric looked around the meadow and the pleasant grasses and small flowers had been replaced by a broken, pock-marked spill of small hills, scattered dirt, and holes to nowhere. "Is that all of them?"

Anika nodded as she looked around, "We should go."

Tyric nodded as he cinched his ax to his body. Pity his sword remained under ground. They strode toward the far side of the meadow.

Part of the hill exposed by a moving tunneler revealed a rocky pocket of a cave. Tyric saw a massive claw-like hand grip the edge of the rock pulling something huge from the hole. He flipped the strap freeing his ax. "We're not done yet."

Chapter VIII: The Korlak

The murky light from the cave pulled back in a curtain as the monster came from the darkness.

"A korlak," Anika breathed.

"A giant of a korlak," said Tyric.

The ruddy red skin of the giant korlak smoldered under the bright sky in grotesque anger. A mottled group of damaged armor slabs hugged its torso in places but dangled from others. The armor and this Korlak had seen heavy battle. Tyric remembered the books in the old armory. Korlak were normally human sized – not like this one. Bony plates protected it with natural armor that filled the spaces between the numerous spikes. The brute snatched boulders strewn about the cave and whirled them at Anika and Tyric. The bounding rocks bounced to either side of the two, one brushing against Tyric's shoulder before the rocks hopped up a little hill of dirt and disappeared into a tunneler hole.

The giant korlak stomped into range and with one fist it struck at them with long rake-like claws that pointed forward from the backs of its fists. Anika jumped into the air backward to avoid the punch. The fist slammed into the dirt. She landed and sprinted at the korlak. The second fist trailed a long sword that Tyric knew would be too heavy for him to lift but the creature swung the sword with ease. Tyric stabbed at the side of the sword with his ax and deflected the stroke into the ground next to him. Tyric brought his ax up and cut through the horny arm of the korlak above the elbow. The korlak bellowed as blood shot across the ground. Anika snatched a long dagger from Tyric's belt and pierced the sword hand. The giant korlak's arm swung wide and close to Anika. She flattened in a small spillway of soft dirt left from a tunneler burrow. Other holes punctured the ground behind Tyric and Anika.

The korlak stabbed its sword at Tyric, but the dagger pinned the sword and its hand at a bad angle and Tyric easily ducked the wide blade. He rushed forward and chopped at the stout thigh. His ax struck deep and hard. Tyric turned his body in the direction to loosen the ax, yanked it free, and struck again into the same slot. His ax sheared through the thigh bone and ripped out more meat from the wound. The korlak toppled, trapping its sword under its flailing body. Tyric jumped onto the monster's chest and hewed with his ax, splitting the face like cord wood. His ax continued down into the stump of the monster's neck, buried in flesh and bone. He rode the flexing muscles bucking like a ship lost at sea in a dangerous red storm.

Anika said, "That one saw real battle."

Tyric reached for his breath, "Like this? This seemed like real battle."

"No, armies clashing. Old wounds and scars show big battles. Magic."

"How do you know this?"

"Servant girls hear things, if one pays attention."

Tyric yanked his dagger from the creature's fist,

"That was not an accidental stabbing. You pinned its whole hand."

"I saw I could help and so I took a chance."

"You need to tell me more about who you really are."

"Not much to know. Just a castle servant. Should we check that cave to make sure no more surprises?"

"Yes." Tyric stalked toward the cave and peered around the edge of the broken rock.

A rough table of logs banded together with coiled grape vines filled half the cave. A wet cave, at least the half not covered by the table showed open to the sky and the elements but remained in enough shadow it never dried. The dry side of the cave housed the table. Upon the table, a dozen gelatinous spheres nestled with grass and rags ringing their bases to keep them from rolling and jostling each other. The eggs shimmered with the same colors as the tunnelers and seemed to move slightly as pebbles dropped into otherwise still ponds, rippling gently in solitude. Trash littered the wet side of the cave and other junk plugged the space under the table. Leaves and dead grass filled the corners and plastered the walls as blown in by the elements. Anika approached the table, nearly shoulder tall to her. She rooted in the debris under the table.

"Shouldn't we look at those eggs? Not the trash pushed under there?"

Anika shrugged, "We can guess what those are, and I want to see what else is here." She pulled at a rotting leather satchel holding moldy cheese and gnarled wood chunks good for a hot fire. Grass stuffing for anything, possibly packing for the eggs. "What was this korlak doing?"

"Looks like some sort of nursery."

"Too temporary here for that," she crouched and went under the table, pushing and pulling at the debris. Rusty iron farm implements, a broken shield and armor.

"Looks like the owner of that armor had the armor peeled off him a piece of the time and then eaten. I'd leave that."

"Good idea." Anika pushed the armor away.

"I'm much more interested in what we do with these eggs than looking in that junk. What if these things hatch?"

"They are not ready yet."

"– What?"

"I mean, if they were going to hatch we'd see something going on, right?"

"They move below the surface like maggots."

"I guess there is nothing here." Anika stepped out from under the table.

Tyric could see passed her shoulder, "What's that?"

Anika looked over her shoulder. Something flashed on the rock under the table. Both of them scrambled over the debris and came to the rock wall.

Tyric grunted, "Just water dripping down from above. We need to kill the eggs."

Anika looked closer at the rock. She took her finger nail and chipped at the flaking black stone. She used her dagger and thrust at the spongy rock. "There is something beyond. The water isn't dripping from above, at least not this side of the wall." The rock crumbled and gave way revealing a small hole, "Look, a room."

Tyric peered through the hole, took his ring, and shined a narrow beam through the opening. He could see a larger chamber.

Anika backed up, "Let's take a look at these eggs now."

Tyric's boot crunched across old steel, crumbly with age. He stooped to pick the object up and bring it to the light. "Look, a broken sword. Old, like from the Great War. I can't make out any blacksmith marks. But the style is of the old Kelvin to the far south."

"The swamps? What is that doing up here?"

"It's old and crumbly but it's from somewhere else. It was just stored here." He closed his eyes and felt with his mind. The magic that Erolok had taught him revealed a fading old power nearly vanquished by rust. "Once a magic sword. Even if I forged it clean and new, the magic is nearly faded."

"Do you think the korlak searched for someone or something? This far into the elven kingdom?"

Tyric tossed the sword to the floor where it thudded from built-up oxides. "More likely deserting a kelvin battle with these prized eggs."

"What do you make of them?" Anika stood on her toes, "Look at how round and how the colors swirl like the skin of the tunnelers." She reached a hand out to touch the nearest one.

"No." Tyric held her hand back.

Anika paused, "Why?"

"The way those things move in there they could hatch any time." Tyric swung his ax. The blade chopped easily through the gelatinous sphere. The contents erupted as if under pressure and a squiggling tunneler the size of Tyric's arm flopped back and forth, jumping and hopping on the banded log table toward the edge. Tyric wrenched the ax around and chopped at the jerking worm. His blade missed it. He wrenched it free of the timber. His boots shuffled in the rubble on the cave floor. He knew if the worm hit the soft dirt floor, it could disappear and grow strong to terrorize this country. Maybe it could track him. The myths of these things told stories of hunting packs sent against King Aleron in the Great War. How long to get to full size? Even this size could take a hand off an arm or burrow through a chest. The thing seemed to grow longer as it curled from side to side, bouncing on the logs. Tyric matched its movements and then struck. His ax split along the tunneler and its motions halted.

"How do we eliminate the other eggs?"

"I guess I'll need your help. I don't want them getting to the dirt."

Anika nodded, "That could be bad."

Tyric climbed on the table and stood next to the nearest egg, "Ready?"

Anika nodded, her dagger prepared for any escapees. Working together, they killed the dozen potential monsters. Tyric jumped from the table and they went to the face of the crumbly shale wall. He picked up a heavy knot of wood with a thick stem of a branch still attached and swung it at the wall. Rock splinters shattered off and tinkled to the floor of the cave. A few solid strikes and a hole opened large enough for his shoulder, then his torso, then enough so they slipped through into the small room.

Stalactites hung from the ceiling, their drippings oozed over the floor and encased much of a pile of shells and beads. Along the top of the pile lay a short sword that shimmered in the light.

Anika reached for the sword.

Tyric stayed her hand, "Could it be trapped?"

"Unlikely. A cave in the middle of the wilderness in the land of elves," she gripped the handle of the sword and lifted the weapon from the shells. She spun the handle in her hand and gripped it tight, testing its balance. A slight smile fluttered across her lips as she looked along the sword in satisfaction.

"You look handy with that sword."

She swished it clumsily back and forth. Then she turned and brought the edge of the sword against Tyric's throat, "I can protect myself, at least as well as a servant girl, and better with this sword."

"I think you have mastered a sword better than any servant girl I've ever seen."

"Don't think too much or I might kill you here."

Tyric put his fingers against the flat of the weapon and pushed the sword away, "You might have a little more trouble than that."

She stepped closer to Tyric, "I'm not so sure." Her eyes kept his. Then she spun the sword around and put it under her belt.

"You're keeping that?"

THE BLUE CRYSTAL

"It's too small for your frame. And it suits me."

"Fine. I have my ax and you've done surprising things with a dagger."

Chapter IX: Plateau Ruins

Tyric pulled himself up the ledge. The wind blew crumbling dust away from his hand as he lifted it to grip another rock. Anika dangled from the wall behind him. Rubble tumbled far below from what had once been a road rising from the plain to the top of the plateau. "When the Shadow Wizard attacked Emperor's Keep he trapped everyone up here by toppling that road."

Anika said, "I remember that story too."

Tyric swung his leg over and pulled himself to the rocks at the top of the plateau. Scrub grasses clung to life on the heat and rock. He looked south and the lakes of Tadur glittered toward the horizon. He saw the spilling homes and shops of the city of Ket. The monastery of Zan huddled atop its rocky thumb of an island. He rolled over to his knees and stood. Anika came to the top of the plateau and crouched, "Something isn't right."

"It should be more than safe, given how hard it is to get up here. It looks the same as when I came here before."

Giant white blocks of broken stone tumbled in twisted, fractured piles, abandoned with the last Great War a thousand years prior. The stories of his childhood flooded back. "The walls were thick and the towers tall. Gold painted the rim of the walls so they glowed at dawn –"

"Yeah, unlikely real gold."

"King Aleron defeated the Shadow Wizard and returned here after disbanding his army."

Anika checked her weapons, "Then the Shadow Wizard appeared in King Aleron's court."

"– And killed him." Tyric moved toward the broken remains of the main gate. Blasted rock lay strewn everywhere while some rocks had seen so much heat they turned to slag and glass. Tyric walked through the main gate and turned to look out over the land. Somehow seeing the main gate from the interior of the keep wedged something free from his memories. He pictured what this place must have looked like then. His ring burned his finger. He nearly tore it off. The blue of the gem swirled like a pool of madness. Flashes struck across his eyes whenever he blinked. Visions showed what the keep had been in its grandeur. Everywhere he looked he saw ruin but closing his eyes, he saw what the place had been. People fled the main gate. The purple lightning struck from the sky and exploded the stone into chunky shrapnel that rained on the fleeing people. The mob raced from the main gate but stopped at the edge of the plateau. The road was gone. Tyric saw them look over their shoulders in fear and terror. A few and then the mass of them dove off the edge to their certain doom.

"What is it?"

"I – I don't know. I saw people die here."

"Ghosts of what happened? Something kept all the thieves away and ghosts could do that."

"I – I'm not sure. This way. This did not happen when I came before."

"Where are you going?"

Tyric blinked, "A flood of people came through here from the court. What magic is here? I can smell them. The sweat and their fear. The overturned cooking braziers of street vendors scorching forgotten food. The acrid lightning blasts gouging the fortress." Tyric walked further toward the interior of the Keep. Anika followed Tyric around, between, and over the broken fragments of stone. Fractured rock that showed the eroded remains of delicate carvings. Tyric stood among fallen columns and roof blocks that lay cut like tunnelers hacked to pieces. He stopped before a pile of thick blocks that sat on fractured tile that still showed a black and white checkerboard pattern from under their edges. Elsewhere the tile had turned to rubble. "We need to go there. A passage goes down."

"How do you know?"

"I don't." Tyric held up his ring to the sunlight. It had calmed and only sparkled now. "Maybe the Elf King cast a spell on me?"

"As if the mad King could remember a spell."

"Then what is drawing me here?"

"That gem of yours?"

"Maybe." Tyric put his arms around the first block that seemed easiest to move.

"You're tipping it." Anika scooped up small shards of stone from the ground to wedge between Tyric's rock and another. Tyric pulled on the rock again. Anika pushed the wedges deeper.

"Stand back." Tyric pulled on the rock until he felt it come to a balance point and then he tipped it out. He jumped back and the rock cracked into the ground. He gripped another rock and tipped that. Anika wedged pieces behind it to give Tyric a break. His shoulders stretched and bunched until he spun another rock away from the pile. Tyric pulled at rocks until his feet became thick and hollow. His shoulders drooped and burned like melted wax. He wanted to rest but something drove him on. Finally, he had a hole opened across the passage wide enough for him to squeeze through.

A voice that Tyric recognized but had not expected, nor heard approach, said, "Good job uncovering that passage for us."

Tyric turned, sweat running into his eyes that he cleared with the back of his leather gauntlet. Where he thought he had glimpsed a single shadow with the voice, he saw Prince Frael flanked by a dozen regular sized korlak. Tyric grabbed Anika and flung her through the hole, backing in behind her. He pushed Anika forward into the dark tunnel.

Anika pushed back, "There could be traps anywhere down here."

"We have a wizard behind us. Move!"

The passage nearly filled across with several cave-ins forcing them to crawl and slide sideways to get beyond them. Tyric used his ring to light their way. He could hear the korlak behind them.

"Which way?" Anika said when the passage forked.

Tyric closed his eyes. An image tugged him, "Right. Go to the right."

They rushed forward and then the passage ended abruptly. They turned and half the korlak sprinted for them. Tyric freed his ax while Anika brought up her sword. She sliced through the first korlak. Anika grabbed a dagger from the korlak she cut down. She spun, kicked a second korlak, and threw the dagger into another korlak's neck.

Tyric hacked into a korlak with his ax and then a second as the first fell in a growl. Tyric sheared through the breastplate of a korlak nearing Anika's side. Tyric's ax flailed into another and Anika struck the last down with her sword. The two pressed forward down the hallway.

Anika ran her fingers over the walls looking for clues. "Are you sure we should have gone to the right?"

"Yes."

Anika pressed against the wall with her hands. She found a loose brick that wobbled. She twisted the face of it and a door slowly opened before them. Crossbow bolts from the korlak splattered across the wall, forcing them to dive through the opening of a passage that went unerringly straight for thirty yards before turning. They peered around the corner and the tunnel continued farther than they could see, but an opening beckoned on the right-hand wall.

The opening went into a large room, sprawled with piles of ancient decayed wood.

The hall continued until a bend in the corridor led to a dead end.

"This is a good escape," said Anika as she pressed the walls looking for anything that might release them.

She found a small crack around a brick. She touched the brick and pressed slowly. The brick gave like pushing against river bottom mud and the wall split aside. The corridor spiraled into the darkness adorned with carvings of dragon scales on the walls and floor. They stepped over the threshold and followed the corridor ahead as it twisted tighter into the earth. A jagged seam in the wall opened as they approached. Beyond loomed a vaulted cavern where columns that once supported the lofty ceiling dripped down in thick frozen stalactites of the drabbest soot – like the great maw of a terrible beast, patiently waiting in the darkness. The cavern smelled of the cool rocky earth tinged with the remains of an ancient fire and another odor they could not place. A chill draft fluttered through the shadows.

Tyric moved into the room. Anika tucked close behind him. They both held their weapons in the uneasy air of the place. "Think this was the chamber where the Shadow Wizard killed King Aleron?"

"Or something."

A skeleton, blackened and charred like the room, clacked out of the shadows and swung a chipped sword at Anika.

Tyric struck at the skeleton with his ax. His weapon thudded against the skeleton's armor plates. Tyric cut at the skeleton's outreaching arm. The blade cut into the leather wrapping the skeleton's forearm, but did not get through the underlying iron bands. The plodding skeleton's heavy blade hammered down on Tyric's shoulder. Tyric spun and returned with a cut from the side.

Anika crouched down as a second skeleton swung a jeweled flail at her head. She grabbed a gold pot half filled with rough cut gems and bowled it into the skeleton's chest. Through the cloud of black dust erupting from the skeleton's armor at the impact, Anika chopped up under the skeleton's leg armor. Energy flowed in the solid old bones. The skeleton rasped a dry scream, but the blade would not come free from where it wedged into the leg! The skeleton wrenched its body to the side and pulled Anika's sword from her hands.

Tyric caught the skeleton's sword against his ax and turned to the side as the skeleton's next strike came across.

Anika dodged her skeleton's lashing flail.

Tyric glanced about, but all he could see were gems and coin, again, spots melted and some not. "No, use that dagger of yours."

"Yeah! You get close to this thing," Anika scrambled away as the flail bounced against a large chest that Anika had been behind, denting the green copper.

Tyric feinted to one side and then fell to the other. He grabbed the handle of his ax tight-in with both hands and sprang up under the skeleton's guard. The ax slid between the layers of armor and scrapped through the parchment dry skin covering the skeleton's belly. The skeleton moaned as the ax continued through the spine, separating the segments.

Tyric wrenched sideways, trying to free his weapon as the skeleton brought the hilt of its sword to bash Tyric's head. Tyric twisted away only to find the skeleton's other hand at his neck.

Anika scooped up a heavy silver chain she found. The flail skeleton moved again to strike. Stepping forward, Anika whipped the chain around the sword as if lashing a boat to a dock cleat. The free ends entwined in her hands, Anika pulled back against the chain, pulling the skeleton forward to the floor, its leg at a wild angle with the sword still stuck in it.

The skeleton's cold smooth fingers closed against Tyric's neck. Tyric released his ax, grabbed his dagger, and plunged it through the leather wraps, between the lower arm bones and twisted. He gripped the dagger with both hands, braced his legs on the skeleton's thigh and wrenched. His neck muscles bulged as he arched his back to counteract the torque on the skeleton arm and the grip at his neck. The bones were not brittle, but ductile, and only bent. Tyric's vision blurred from the strain and lack of air. He knew he did not have much time left. With a last effort, he bounced on the dagger twice and the third time heaved against the dagger's handle. The skeleton bones yielded and fractured at last! Tyric fell to the floor, rolling away from the skeleton. Still the skeleton's fingers crushed his throat!

The second skeleton, orienting itself from its new position on the floor, reached up and yanked the chain. Anika's hands were too entwined in the chain and she fell toward the skeleton. The skeleton swung the flail and caught Anika against her ribs and her armor padding, the blow spinning her around. Anika worked at getting out of the chain as the skeleton dropped the flail, ponderously regained its feet and reeled the chain, dragging Anika closer.

Tyric forced the fingers of his hands behind the

crushing skeleton grip, but failed. His thoughts came slower. Through the bare branches of a burned forest, he saw the sun fade into the white disk of the moon against a jet sky. The moon even faded and Tyric reached for it. His mind flailed a last throw and commanded his fingers, too thick and fat to fit. His hands that worked the forge bellows, hammered hot steel, that wrenched on stubborn bolts, and chopped down thick trees tugged at the bones squeezing his neck. The blackness wanted to claim him but his fingers latched at the edges of the skeleton's grip. He locked his wrists and peeled the skeleton's fingers. They lifted and he tore at them. Air! He pulled. His knees faded and he stumbled to keep upright. His fingers slipped on the old bones and Tyric dug his fingers in again. This time he hooked the skeleton's thumb and wrenched it out where he worked his other hand behind the remaining skeleton digits. He tore it away! The hand fluttered around on the ground but could do no damage if left alone. Tyric sucked in the musty burned air and it seemed like the clearest elixir from the fresh deep woods. The skeleton ambled toward him, brandishing the broken stumps of its arm bones as jagged fire pokers.

    Anika struggled with the chain, it wrapped tightly about her thumbs and wrists. The skeleton pulled the chain closer, the next clasp of its hand would reach Anika's arm. Anika rolled to the side, getting one hand free, she slipped between the skeleton's legs. She gripped its ankle and pulled hard. Even with all the armor, the skeleton was light and fell forward easily. The skeleton tipped itself back to its knees and then to its feet. In those few seconds, Anika freed herself from the chain and fled.

Tyric charged his skeleton, his ax swinging. The stump of the skeleton's shattered arm jabbed against Tyric's armor and into Tyric's shoulder. Tyric squeezed his hand around the skeleton arm and crunched down on the skeleton's knee with his ax. He pushed the skeleton away to stumble about reorienting itself. Tyric shambled toward the skeleton and swatted at it with a powerful ax stroke. The blade cut through the armor across the skeleton's shoulder and sliced down through ribs, but then he could not pull his ax free! Tyric's ax stuck fast! He spun about, the skeleton flipping like a doll at the end of his ax, his strength flailing the skeleton into the air and smashing the skeleton against the dusty melted treasure. He could not free his ax. He jumped with his boots on the skeleton's chest and bounced up and down like a mad carnival ride. Only a few of the skeleton's bones cracked under the barrage. Tyric did not relent. He pummeled the skeleton until the ribs holding his ax separated from the rest of the skeleton's frame and he leaped back, careful of not touching the ragged ends of the skeleton to anything.

Tyric watched the mauled skeleton pull itself up. So much of its scaffolding did not work anymore that it struggled to stand. Tyric looked around for a sizable chest that appeared less damaged than others. He reached over the top of a suitable container and ripped the top from the chest. Inside the chest gold coins, rings, and jewels gleamed. The treasure wrapped in the chest sparkled like wondrous stars in contrast with the soot encrusted and half melted treasure remains about the rest of the chamber. Tyric took his ax stuck to the skeleton pieces and jammed the whole mess into the treasure chest and scrubbed it back and forth.

Tyric pulled his ax from the treasure scattering loose rings and coins into the air. At the end of his ax was now a massive golden club. Tyric snorted and ran at the skeleton that had regained its footing and hobbled toward him. Tyric moved forward, holding the golden ball out to his side. When he neared, he swung the ball around and pounded it down on top of the skeleton. The force of the blow folded the skeleton like a fan-fold paper screen amid creaking and splintering bones. Tyric rolled away from the debris, fearful of any shrapnel sticking to him.

Anika moved toward Tyric, her skeleton limping close behind her with Anika's sword still stuck in its leg. Anika stumbled and fell to the floor. Pain from her ribs thrust through her body. She turned quickly to see her foot had caught a loop of strap from Tyric's pack. She rummaged through it as she moved ahead of the skeleton.

Tyric trudged forward with the ball of gold nearing Anika and the second skeleton. He saw how she readied to click flint across the steel, intent on showering an oily rag with sparks. Tyric turned around, realizing the cause of the charred and melted treasure, not from a protecting fiend but treasure hunters trying to destroy these skeletons.

"No!" Tyric ordered.

Anika froze.

Tyric rushed the skeleton shambling after Anika. He hammered it with the golden ball. The skeleton bent and sprawled back so that the ball smashed its legs. The gold ball became stuck to the skeleton's legs, which also adhered to the treasure melted to the floor.

The skeleton struck at Tyric's shoulder.

Anika approached Tyric and the skeleton. She dropped the oil and striker and snatched a melted silver harp from nearby. A grunt and she smashed it against the skeleton. The harp bounced. Tyric picked up the harp with his free hand and crushed it against the skeleton's shoulder. Pieces of skeleton armor fell away showing the gleaming bones beneath. Tyric dropped the harp.

"Cover this thing with treasure."

Anika looked for anything big and loose.

Tyric used the harp and smashed it against the skeleton. The skeleton reeled back and Tyric struck it again but this time he left the harp across the skeleton and leaned his boot on the harp pinning the skeleton down.

Anika found a large iron shield. She dragged the torn panel across the scrabble to Tyric. He pulled the shield over the skeleton and stomped his boot down. Skeleton bones crackled and a few broke.

Tyric said, "Find me that mace or something like it but heavier." He kicked repeatedly against the shield.

Anika ran to the edge of darkness in the room and searched wide. Most everything that looked useful had melted into the rest of the treasure. Then she saw an iron bar topped with a war maul. A hammer for the blacksmith! She could not lift it so she dragged it across the uneven floor. Rust flaked off its corners as it scraped silvery-gold gouges through the soot. It came easier across the flat pool of solidified metal marked with their footprints like black snow on a shimmering frozen lake.

Tyric snatched the hammer handle from Anika. He saw the metal and artisanship of the hammer matched the shield. Both centuries old. The hammer came down upon the shield and crushed the skeleton behind it. Each time he mashed the shield and broke the skeleton into smaller pieces the more the shield glued to the floor. He hammered the shield nearly flat. Sticky glue seeped from its edges.

Tyric wrenched his ax free. He took a bag from his pack and dropped the whole mess into the bag. "I'm hoping fire can burn that off. I hope I don't burn off the heat treating in the process."

"We could do that now."

"No. Did you sniff the air?"

"No. I don't smell anything, except this soot."

"It's faint, but I think some sort of explosive gas is in here. No fires."

"Thanks for stopping me with the sparks. I see a passage over there."

A charcoal burned barrel tipped over showing the remains of ornate swords. Tyric pulled at them, "Most of these are ornamental weapons, melted together or bad steel." He kicked at the edge of the barrel, "The fire preserved the wood. And looks like a few of the steel blades might still hold their edge." He dropped a melted mass of the swords to the floor. He pushed aside several loose swords and picked up an ugly looking blade, "This is the best of the lot."

"That doesn't look like much of a sword."

Tyric dug in his pack and used a patch of leather and a small coil of wire. He cut the charred handle from the sword and wrapped it new. He squeezed his hand around it and swung it in the air, "It will do until I can free my ax." He looped a strip of leather cord around it under the cross-guard to his belt. He did the same with a second sword for Anika. With a nod, they entered the passage.

The smell of the gas became stronger as they continued through the passage. The way curled and descended.

"Stop!" Anika said. Her arm holding across Tyric's chest.

She picked up a small rock and tossed it ahead of them on the floor of the corridor. The rock disappeared through the floor ahead of them. They could hear it faintly striking a wall, then another and eventually it must have hit bottom, as they heard it no more – or the rock still fell.

Tyric scanned the walls. He saw a string of iron spikes hammered into the wall with wire tied between them like a musical instrument. The centuries old wire and spikes revealed rotting corrosion. "Someone traversed that pit." Tyric felt cautiously for the edge of the real floor and the beginning of the illusion.

Anika walked back up their passage and found a few more loose rocks at the edges of the walls. She returned and tossed them out until they saw the far edge. "The spikes and wires go just beyond the far edge. Someone solved this problem a long time ago."

"They searched for more than treasure to go this far."

"What did the Elf King send you here for? And why is your ring glowing?"

"You haven't told me about how you use a sword so well." Tyric glanced at his ring, remembering the words from the Elf King that it would glow when he neared the dragon egg. He searched in his pack. He took out his own spikes, fluted so light yet still strong. He put the spike against the wall and swung his small brass hammer at it. "I only brought rope so we won't get across on so fancy of a conveyance."

"That's fine. You think more korlak are getting sent down here?"

"I expect it."

"Then don't leave the rope when we get across."

On the far side of the pit, Tyric yanked the free end of the rope, it untied the knot, and he coiled it back up. They continued ahead. The passage turned and ended.

Six long dead and weary plunderers lay on the floor. Charred and scorched. Tyric inspected the bodies, "Elves. Their armor style is centuries old. Maybe still left over from the Great War."

"They escaped the fire and died here, fearing to go back?"

"Or died from some trap we haven't found yet."

Anika searched the walls methodically, "I don't see anything except these gouges and where they hammered at the walls with their spikes."

Tyric looked at the tools and he saw the heavy wear, "They must have starved here trying to scrape through. Everything is blunt, not chipped and bent. Like …" Tyric looked at more of the gouges in the walls and matched up a few of the discarded tools. "Like they rubbed the rock rather than striking against it."

"They learned of the gas from their fight with the skeletons."

"And would not want to strike sparks."

Anika sucked her breath, "And we just hammered in those spikes!"

"We placed those in cracks and hammered metal on metal, but that hammer of mine is brass so it would not spark either."

"Why did they think something might be here? They could have gone back across the pit."

"Something kept them here. Maybe the skeletons stood at the far edge?"

Anika searched the bodies but anything useful had rotted and gone. She stood and looked at the walls. "I just don't see anything."

"They did not find anything on the walls." Tyric looked up, "But what about the ceiling?"

Anika spun about, "Lift me up." Tyric put his hands about her waist and lifted her to his shoulders. "Ow!"

Tyric said, "Sorry, forgot about your ribs."

She rubbed her side and steadied herself with a hand on Tyric's head while she climbed higher. She balanced with her feet on his shoulders. "Move slowly to the left wall and I'll start searching there. I'm high enough standing on your shoulders that I can put my hands flat against the ceiling." She searched the stone blocks for cracks and any other telltale sign. "Move to the right a half step." She searched more of the ceiling. "This will take a long time."

"I think we have a bit. At least until the korlak get brave again, or Prince Frael decides to investigate. Don't hurry or anything. My shoulders can take it."

"Big broad shoulders," Anika giggled. "Left now."

"I found something. A rectangle of rock ringed by another larger rectangle set in this block that crosses the ceiling."

"What do you think it might do if you press it?"

"Open a hidden door." She saw the face of the inner-most block showed small gouges as if someone pressed it before with a long spear. "If you know this is here, like someone must have, you thrust a spear up here and bump it."

"Or it drops a block crushing us."

"Maybe not with the skeletons down there."

"Or it seals off the tunnel trapping us here like these plunderers."

"They left the wires across the pit."

"They might have been in a hurry."

"Or someone came down here and then left. They sealed rocks over the entrance."

"And left the treasure?"

"Maybe they had something more pressing on their mind?"

Tyric looked about the passage. "We're fugitives; a

wizard sits at the doorstep like a cat waiting for two mice to escape from the wall. Press it and we'll fight whatever comes."

Anika took a deep breath and pressed the block.

The block pulled into the ceiling. A grinding noise thundered through the rock and increased in speed leaving a shaft going up into darkness. The grinding continued.

Tyric squeezed Anika's thighs just above her knees and set her on the floor. They stepped back carefully toward the bend in the passage.

"Look at that."

The ceiling split open and a block dropped, moved forward, then another block dropped into place. When the rumbling stopped a stairway beckoned to them.

Tyric held his hand out, "Up the stairs."

"To the dragon's lair?"

The top of the stairs opened into a wide room with a dais at the far end. A round orb glowed with an inner light sitting on top of the dais. The two strode across the floor with cautious footsteps.

"Look at how all the candelabras and small statues are scattered around the dais and this globe is here?"

"That's not a globe." Tyric put his hand near the orb. He could feel the throbbing heat coming from the glow inside. "This is what the Elf King sent me for."

"A crystal ball?"

"No. A dragon's egg."

"Dragons?"

"That's what the King asked me to find. I thought it might not exist – you've seen what he writes on his papers. Why might anything be true that he said? Since it was true, why is this here?" Tyric dumped out his pack and stuffed a measure of his blanket into the bottom, and then he carefully lifted the egg from the dais and put it in his pack. He wrapped the blanket all around and over the egg. He slid the protective metal sheets he carried along the sides of the pack to protect the egg further. Then he took another blanket and wrapped the outside of the pack. He swung it on his back and filled his pockets with things he thought they might need soon, abandoning the rest.

Anika pointed to a scrawled note gouged into the wall behind the dais, "What do you think this means?"

... Six others stand in one great hall
The same and different one and all
Two have fallen, four yet might
As another battle are they to fight
In wars against a Shadow great
The empires old he felled in hate...

Tyric looked at the writing and said, "Just a fragment of a longer riddle."

"Have you seen it before?"

"No. Probably a wizard looking for fame."

"Whoever put the egg here must have written those words."

"Perhaps."

"You are important to whatever this is about."

Tyric laughed, "Right. A blacksmith. That kind of stuff is for wizards and heroes." Tyric's face went serious, "What do you know that makes you think I am tied to that?"

"I – I don't know. You are here getting a dragon's egg, sent by a king –"

"– An insane king."

"– Still, a king gave you an important mission. We actually find a dragon's egg, and we have assassins, wizards, and tunnelers chasing us. I may have gotten cross-wise of gossip in court but nothing like this." Her eyes widened, "As if you have a Destiny."

"I don't have time for any talk of Destiny. I'm just a blacksmith and maybe contributing to this piece of it but that's it. I don't know where you get that idea."

Anika looked like she wanted to argue more, but just nodded.

Tyric lifted his ax while the other held the sword. "We have enough of a challenge to get passed the wizard without breaking this egg."

"Why is Prince Frael here? They would send the guard to find us and if a prince came with the guard, it would be Prince Elraf. And why does Prince Frael have korlak?"

"Probably politics going on between the two. Each striving for the throne. I hate politics." He did not add, *Especially when the Elf King told me a new war is brewing, confirmed by this riddle.*

Chapter X: A Wizard Waits

"They've been busy," Anika said as she pulled back from the corner of the passage. "They cleared the rest of the rocks from the exit."

Tyric stared at the crossbow bolt wedged in the passage wall across from them. "The korlak range tested their crossbow sights already after reducing our cover. Too bad that huge iron shield is glued to the floor. Handy using it for our escape."

"They don't know we are here, yet."

Tyric said, "I don't want to waste our surprise. Let's go back to the treasure room. Maybe something will spark our interest."

"How heavy are those elf skeletons? A few had armor and we could use them as shields."

"Awkward. We'd have to get them across the pit. I want to take another look at the treasure room."

Tyric dumped the lid from a tin chest onto the ground, "That's it. Nothing else looks like it could be a shield."

"They are all tiny." Anika said, "How are we going to stitch them together?"

"Like this." Tyric used his little hammer and stretched out a chunk of gold he broke off the floor. Soon he had a strap. He sectioned coins protected in a chest into rivets that he used to hold the various plates and ornate pot lids and flattened kettles together. He hefted the finished shield. "It's a heavy one but this should stop all the crossbow bolts farther than ten feet away. The bolt stuck in the hallway is a light crossbow bolt which matches what a moving gang like that would carry."

Just before dawn, Tyric nudged Anika awake, "Ready?"

"Surprising we spent so much of the night down here."

Tyric lifted the wall shield. They rushed around the corner and up the ramp to the surface.

Peels of alarm broke across the rubble above the passage. A barrage of crossbow bolts struck their shield. The two reached the opening of the passage and explosive fire burst around them. Tyric felt his ring dissipating the magic and shielded Anika since she remained close enough. Tyric could not see the wizard. New projectiles struck against the shield. Tyric had worked building several fast firing crossbows as a challenge and admired their impressive reload speeds. The tips of the crossbow bolts wiggled through the back layers of the shield as Tyric ran forward. Tyric and Anika split to either side of the shield and scooped their weapons into the frantically reloading korlak. Tyric killed three and Anika two before the korlak realized their danger and drew their swords.

Tyric killed four and Anika the last two so they could turn and confront new attackers rushing from the sides. Tyric grabbed the handle of his ax-club and spun the sword in his other hand. The korlak neared and he sliced through them, bashed the club over more, and strode into the mass of korlak swirling around them. He kept Anika protected behind him as he clubbed or cut through the unending tide of korlak. Keeping Anika in that position also reminded him not to expose his back and the nested egg.

Silence hovered over them after the last korlak crumpled to the dust between the rubble. Sweat dripped from Tyric's face and stuck his back to his armor. His breath came hard through the silence. "Where is the wizard?"

Anika said, "I did not see him when we came out. He must have left the korlak to take care of us."

"No. He's still there somewhere. Waiting to attack us again."

"We can't stay here. The guard will find us if we pause."

"And the wizard will track us too."

"Best for us to move."

"We have enough rope to climb down any side of the plateau."

"Yes, better than using the same path we came here. The wizard or the guard likely waits for us."

Tyric walked to the north side where a few scrub bushes dotting the rim when they first looked for a way to the top. Anika stayed with him. "Powerful magic pulled this place apart," Tyric said as they climbed over and went around what might have been granaries and storage bunkers for the fortress. The scrub bushes waved to them through a large split in the crumbled outer wall. Tyric looked at his ax and at the scrub. He set down his weapons and lifted a fractured log of a larger bush that fell years ago.

"What are you doing?" Anika sat on a chunk of rounded over granite.

"I'd like my ax better than this gaudy club."

"I don't know, it sparkles in the sunlight and makes you look like a King with a scepter."

"It's a tool, not something for show. A tool needs to work." He dropped more pieces of wood. From his pouch, he took a flint and steel and drove sparks into tinder.

"They will see the fire and find us."

"I've built so many fires I cannot count and I intend a smokeless burn. This wood with the coarse bark burns fast; the smoother limbs will burn slow but hot." He flipped his encrusted ax over in his hands looking at the clump of debris clutching it like barnacles, "I think I need a hot fire to burn this skeleton off."

"That is a lot of treasure, just on that ax."

"The treasure is tempting but it's just metal to be used to make things. The treasure will only slow us down. Now that we have two elven princes chasing us."

Anika nodded.

The fire came up and Tyric held the ax head over the hottest flames watching how the treasure roasted into slag and then slipped off the faces of the ax. The skeleton residue smoldered and bubbled like hot thick grease in a frying pan. Tyric used a shard of granite he found nearby to scrape at the stronger lumps but he soon had the faces cleared. A gold wash skimmed across the ax, fused to the steel. Tyric laughed, "Look, I have a gaudy ax anyway. A good sharpening and polish will remove most of it though." He leaned the ax against a block of stone and collected new green branches from the bushes. He came back to the fire and set them next to it. The nearest leaves curled away from the heat. "We'll place our ropes and then create a little distraction."

"Is that wise? We're climbing down this side of the plateau."

"We'll be down and gone by the time they climb up here or the wizard finds the fire," Tyric took his big rope and a small thin string. He walked to the rim of the plateau and tossed the coils over the edge. Then he tied the climbing rope to the stoutest bush. He tied the small line to the big rope's pig-tail hanging out of the knot. He laid the little rope far to the side of the climbing rope. He gripped the big rope in his gauntleted hands. "You want to go first or second?"

"I'll go first." Anika pulled out a patch of leather to wrap the rope and put her thumbs through little cuts in it. She backed out over the edge and kicked out from the wall. Tyric watched her descend. Then he ran back to the branches and kicked them into the fire. A burst of smoke filled the sky at first like a mushroom then a long heavy stream as the leaves burned black. Tyric gripped the rope and kicked over the edge. His gloves burned as he slid down. He squeezed his grip and slowed his slide to the ground. A quick tug of the small rope and the two ropes came down. Anika wound the lighter line while Tyric wound the heavier rope. They ran in a crouch through the tall grasses and light scrub that covered the landscape on this side of the plateau. They paused under a sprawling solitary oak tree but did not see any movement behind them or as far as the horizon. They moved again. When the sun neared setting, they came upon a group of trees clumping together. They pushed forward. Eventually they came to a small swampy area ringed with a small forest. They skirted the dark water reflecting the red boiling sky. They came on a thick group of elm trees where the darkness deepened. They paused and rested.

"We'll camp here tonight," Tyric said.

Anika pulled out her blanket and curled up between a pair of tree roots, "Do you want first watch or should I?"

Tyric said, "I'm still awake. I'll switch in a few hours. Get your sleep." Tyric sat between tree roots against a tree opposite Anika. He watched the night and listened. His pack with the egg sat next to his knee but in a protected hollow of the roots where he could feel the pack's presence. His ax lay across his thighs. He wanted his blanket out of the pack to keep the biting insects away but he did not want to disrupt the careful placement of the egg wrapped in his blanket.

Frogs croaked nearer to the water, interspersed with the cricket songs. A loud mosquito buzzed his ear. Tyric brushed at it with his fingers, spinning the insect away with the air turbulence, but it soon returned. He snapped his fingers into a fist around the noise and it stopped. He squeezed his fingers, flexing them to crush the insect and then he opened his hand trying to catch his palm in a thin beam of starlight. A dark smear marked his palm.

"There you are," whispered a voice from the darkness.

Tyric launched to his feet, his ax in one hand and the sword in the other. Light filled a ring around them that Tyric put up without thinking about it. Prince Frael walked toward him, mostly covered by a black cloak. The wizard brought his hand up and purple lightning shocked down from clouds that appeared overhead and sank like a fog among the tree trunks. The lightning reached for Tyric but it dissipated as it neared him. The wizard looked puzzled for a moment. Then streaks of fire burst from his other hand and those too faded as they came to touch Tyric. Tyric swung at the wizard with the sword. The cloak on the wizard hardened like a shell where he struck. He brought his ax around and it clanged against the cloak but marked it. Tyric threw the sword back and it stuck in the tree. He gripped his ax with both hands and spun the blade with a cut that went from low to high, catching the wizard's chest. The cloak fabric tore slightly but the force of his hit picked the wizard up and tossed him a dozen yards across the forest. The wizard hit the ground and tumbled until his hands gripped small saplings struggling under the shadow of the older trees. The wizard touched the clasp on his cloak and whirled it off into the air where it spun until the breeze dissipating the fog caught it and lofted it open with the snap of a sail. The fabric thickened and dropped abruptly to the ground as it transformed into a very real and heavy black dragon. The monster's thick legs flexed as its weight sunk in the moist soil and leaves. It uncoiled its head and roared with a breath that reeked of the dead. It whipped its thick tail at him. Tyric jumped and sliced with his ax through the scales and through the bone of the dragon's tail.

The dragon scooped its tushes into the ground, shoveling the black soil at Tyric in a blinding wall of debris. He spun back as the dirt pounded against him. When he turned back, the dragon's snout opened and blasted a wide spray of acid. Tyric dove to the ground behind a tree. The acid ate through part of the tree and burned through the leaves, twigs, and other ground litter.

The head of the dragon snaked around the tree. It reached around the opposite side with a talon. The dragon snatched Tyric in its claw and pulled him back, opening jaws full of long serrated teeth intending to bite his head off. Tyric pushed against one claw with his hand, forcing it open, when he had his ax free he wheeled his arm around and chopped the ax through the dragon's wrist. Tyric fell to the ground. The bounce on the ground sprung open the other talons, releasing him.

The dragon shook its head and limped closer to Tyric who stepped back deeper into the forest, drawing it away from Anika who he saw wisely surveying the situation from behind a tree. The dragon wove its head back and forth to get a better angle. Acid burst from its mouth. Tyric pulled himself behind a tree. The acid cut deep into the tree and it leaned toward the dragon. The creaking fall alerted the dragon and it stepped aside as the tree toppled to the ground. The dragon's eyes tracked Tyric. Tyric climbed on top of the fallen trunk. He ran down its length and up a branch that took him above the ground. He jumped, landing on the end of another branch that flexed down and then back up, launching him into the air. He landed on the dragon's back.

Tyric swung his ax down against the dragon's spine where the quick blade burst through and down into ribs. The dragon bellowed. It shrieked. Tyric jumped from the broken beast to the leaf covered forest floor. The dragon's reflexes mindlessly thrashed and clawed into the dirt, its tail whipping back and forth between two hickory trees, beating bark from their trunks. The bark spun about the air in a swirling dust cloud maintained by the dragon's wings beating the air while the legs kicked.

The dragon raised its head toward the sky and bellowed. Tyric rushed at the dragon and swung his ax through the base of the dragon's neck. Tyric kept running and leaned against the far side of a thick beech tree. Acid poured out of the cut as the dragon died, its head beating against the ground until it finally stilled. Tyric looked around the edges of the tree for the wizard.

A clap of thunder and lightning struck at Tyric that brightened the forest and he saw the wizard casting another spell. The purple lightning fizzled as it reached him. Tyric ran at the wizard. Tyric heard a different cracking tone. He looked up and saw a tree splinter above him into spears and clubs of wood falling toward him. Tyric slid under a half rotted log while the debris rained down around him. The ground under Tyric rumbled and crevices opened from which scorpions, snakes, and poisonous spiders boiled out. Tyric rolled away from under the log and came at the wizard.

The wizard pulled a long slim rapier with flames burning at its sides. He whipped it across the air and jabbed it at Tyric. Tyric blocked the tip with his ax but the light and fast moving rapier pierced his shoulder between the plates of his armor with a burning hole. Tyric stepped back as if he could escape the heat searing his flesh. He lunged and blocked the rapier with his ax, then thrust it forward. The blades of his ax slipped down the rapier and his strength pushed the basket guard against the wizard's chest. He pushed down on the ax handle and the blade rotated and cut into the wizard's chest. Tyric lifted his foot and kicked the wizard's knee, feeling the crunch of the joint. His fist came up and smashed the wizard's nose. The wizard fell away.

The wound in Tyric's shoulder flashed like a forge fire. He stumbled. His eyes blinked and he saw two or three wizards holding their bloody faces and turning around to limp at him with their rapiers. Tyric could not tell which was real. He blinked again, the burn from his wound increasing and the wizards multiplied. The trees multiplied. He shook his head but the visions only multiplied again. The wizards stumbled toward him; any one of them could have the real rapier. Tyric swung his arm at the wizards that pestered his face like uncountable insects. Tyric swung his ax madly at any of the rapiers that came near but he touched nothing. Then a burning came to his arm. He raised his gauntleted hand and gripped the sword. He leaned forward while he bent the sword with his thumb. Tyric shrugged his shoulder to pull the sword tip from his arm. The wizard looked in fear as he bent the sword tip with his gauntleted hand and curved the point at the wizard. The wizard forgot about Tyric's ax that flashed across and cut through his forearm. The wizard shrieked and flailed his arms until he gripped the bleeding stump. Still surrounded by an army of wizards, Tyric moved toward the wailing one. Tyric raised his ax as he came near. The wizards unfurled a flag and rolled onto it. The device lifted the wizard up between the tree trunks and flew him away above the forest canopy.

Tyric stood on his wobbly legs thinking of the wizard as the trees crowded around him. He wanted to lie down but feared that would be his grave. He blinked and listened to the forest. His body urged him to lie down and sleep but he focused his mind to think. The wizard. The dragon.

Where is Anika? Is she safe? ... Is the egg safe?

Tyric stumbled for their camp. He relied on touching the trees and listening to the sounds of the forest to find his way there.

Chapter XI: Missing Egg

The effects of the sword had worn off by the time Tyric found the group of elms he and Anika used. He must have wandered in delirium for a portion of his search. He found the marks where Anika hid behind the tree during his fight with the dragon. He found her pack dumped out and his pack was gone with the egg.

Did she take the egg to the Elf King herself? Did she betray Tyric to his enemies? Tyric packed their gear and searched for her. He found her footprints leading north. He hefted his pack and followed her trail. "Anika, you're running fast and keeping a strong pace. Why are you not trying to hide your path?"

Tyric increased his stride. He found where she forded a small stream and stopped to rest for a moment, and then ran on. None but he chased her. The realization sank in. She used him to get the egg. Tyric's anger mounted. An insane king sent him on a dangerous mission, befriended by a thief, hunted by the king's son for murders he did not commit in saving the King, attacked by the wizard prince with a troop of korlak.

Tyric paused. He looked around the woods filled with happy chirping birds and humming bees that float between flowers spilling down their vines between a pair of willows. He looked back along the path that brought him here. He looked forward along Anika's path. Betrayed and abandoned. He knew he could be a blacksmith in any town in the kingdom. He could start in the city of Ket, go west to Levet Fortress, or even see the great city of Vatkatal in the far south. Stories said the beaches of Kytran Bay are nice all year long. What did he need with these elves and their games? The words of the Elf King returned to his mind about the need for that dragon in the coming war. Evil encroached upon the land and the world will change. Evil will spoil the beaches of Kytran Bay unless stopped. Tyric looked along Anika's path.

Where are we going, Anika?
What will I do when I find you?

Chapter XII: Murder of Madness

"My son." King Ek opened his eyes and blinked in the sharp motes of light slowly circling Prince Frael, even though he set a small sealing candle on the nightstand with a flame wiggling in the draft like a worm.

"Father – good that you are awake." He pulled the drape further back from the side of the bed. The night air came crisp through the open castle window and the candle danced stronger. No sounds filtered up from outside at this late hour. "I want you to sign this."

The King squinted at the parchment his son held before him. An inkwell and a freshly sharpened quill sat at the bedside next to the anxious flame. "I wondered when you or your brother might come with something like this. You must have made two trips into my chamber to bring these supplies."

Prince Frael said, "I thought I should give courtesy in letting you see it, first."

"You know I have stayed because neither of you are fit for the throne."

"Not as fit as a King that struggles to remain sane during court? A King that scribbles nonsense while the kingdom suffers? While your subjects drift not knowing if they will thrive or if their families will remain safe?"

"All that stuff is nonsense anyway. There are larger threats to the kingdom." His eyes glanced at the stump of his son's wrist, "What happened to your arm?"

"Tyric the blacksmith used his ax."

"You must have given him good reason? It's a fresh wound."

"Not fresh enough that easy healing can restore it. Soon though."

"That's too bad." The King looked out the window. He saw several bats swooping outside the window catching insects. He often watched the bats thinking that must be what the dragon battles looked like in the Old War, the few that remained recorded in the old archives. "Did our blacksmith have any treasure with him?"

"He had that egg you sought to keep secret all these years."

The King smiled.

"Here, take the quill and sign."

The King bent the paper toward his son, "The rest of the writing looks just like mine. Why did you not also sign my name?"

"I thought you might appreciate the chance to sign it."

The King signed the document, he wondered about putting another statement in cryptic code but he knew his mental reputation would keep investigators from digging too deeply. A tactical error. He handed the document to his son, "But he eluded you?"

"He roams free, yes." The wizard dripped candle wax on the document and lifted his father's hand to press the signet ring into the cooling wax. He let his father's hand fall back to the bedding. "However, I ensured he did not keep the egg. I wait for its arrival even now."

The King's face drooped, "He will reclaim it."

"But what did you tell him to do with it?"

"I asked him to bring it to me."

"You did not tell him the rest of the legends? The legends that are coming true?"

"I only told him enough to ensure the safety of that egg. I knew the Shadow Wizard wants it. There are too few dragons left in the world but even rarer among the dragons is the breed in that egg."

"This is fortunate. The blacksmith has little incentive to chase the egg, and with news of your death, he will abandon the project out of concern that Prince Elraf hunts him still." The wizard laid the scroll on the bedding and unlatched a small case of his father's that he returned. When the case struck the bedding, it bounced up and the lid flipped open. Six of the deadly-poisonous dark-tread scorpions from the far southern Swamps of Kal scampered across the bedding. Without deliberation, they stung King Ek from the world.

The elf, that would be king before the next night, blew out the little red candle. He smiled and walked from his father's chambers. The Shadow Wizard had promised him one of the Shadow Staves from the Old War. Prince Frael knew his actions gave him the power of the kingdom but also the only way to save the Enkarian Elves in the coming war. Dangerous times did indeed lie ahead.

"You have told no one?" Prince Elraf said.

The elderly elf cowered before him, his dirty broken teeth only glowed in the lamplight because they were wet, "Sir, I saw it happen and came looking for you with the urgent news."

"How did you see it?"

"I walk the wall at night –"

"After the beer or the brothel?"

"Ye – Yes, my Prince. The air was cool and I watched the bats feeding. A thick camp of bats busied themselves outside your father's window or I would have missed seeing the candle and the wizard lights. The air was so still I could hear many of their words. I stayed, in hiding, until your father's staff found him and the guard rushed in and investigated. When I heard they believed his death a suicide, I knew I must find you with the truth."

"Guards!"

"I tell you the truth!"

"I know, unfortunately." Prince Elraf sliced his curved dagger across the elf's throat and plunged it through his heart. The body slumped to the ground.

The guard pushed through the tent flap with his sword half drawn, "Yes, Prince?"

Prince Elraf rubbed a rag along his dagger and touched at a few spots of blood on his robe, "This elf told me treasonous lies and attacked me. Please dispose of the body."

"Yes ... Sir."

Chapter XIII: Evidence of Death

Tyric followed Anika's path ahead through pale green ferns that lead up a small shadowed hill under spruce trees. The fern's wet leaves brushed his legs and the scent of pine pleasantly filled the air. He crested the small hill and found the remains of a battle with mountain dogs on the other side.

Four brutish mountain dogs lay scattered on the hill. Blood, dog's blood by the look of everything, coated the flattened ferns in recent gouts of red. Anika's footprints marked the circling paw prints of the beasts as they lusted and lunged for her. The dogs died slowly, still attacking with cut legs and snouts from her sword and dagger. A few of her strikes were quick and opportunistic as the monsters closed on her, but he saw how they also sported more surgical wounds that dropped them in place. A piece of her shirt snagged on the tooth of one dog that must have gotten very close. No blood marred its pattern. He circled the battle scene in larger loops looking for any other artifacts, finding where she cleaned her blade against the softer belly fur of her last kill. The only other significant detail he found were Anika's footsteps as she walked further into the pines and ferns.

Tyric paused, "Who are you, Anika? You are more than you seem, at every turn." He dug into his pouch and brought up the lightning bolt ring, the red ruby sparkled in the light as if it too was angry about the lies. *Are you one of them?*

Chapter XIV: Prince Ambush

"Hello, Tyric." Prince Elraf stepped from behind a thick hickory tree.

Tyric looked up from Anika's foot print, fresh in the soft leaf bed between a pair of rocks. He saw how her running stride kept going straight ahead as far has he could see in the trees beyond the Elf Prince. Tyric stood up from his kneel.

"Keep your hands where we can see them," said four guards that floated into sight from behind other trees around him.

"We've watched you for the last hour. You mustn't forget we hunt you, even while you follow another's trail. Whom do you follow? Is it that girl? Did she leave you after a quarrel? Did she break your heart and you wish to mend it?"

Tyric heard other guards from deeper among the trees approach. His ear counted them up to ten guards now.

The Prince said, "I see your ears counting your odds. Don't forget the half dozen in the trees with drawn crossbows. Now toss that sword and ax I see you carrying to the dirt, and slowly."

Tyric drew his sword with excruciating slowness. He held it out at the end of his outstretched arm horizontal with the ground. He watched Prince Elraf's eyes lighten as Tyric opened his palm letting the sword fall toward a pile of leaves the wind had mounded up and kept dry since last season.

Tyric ratcheted his movement spinning to his left. His ax free in his hand. The blade caught the first guard by surprise and dropped him to the dirt before his sword nestled into the leaves. The promised crossbow bolts pelted Tyric's armor but from the feel of their strikes, he guessed only light crossbows with limited range, but a fast reload. His ax struck another guard down. He curled around a cluster of trees growing from an ancient rotted stump knowing the scrub shielded him from the archers. Climbing down from their perches for better aim would give him precious time and distance.

A sword whipped through the air and bit the trunk of one of the trees. Tyric beat down Prince Elraf's sword, swung in with his free hand, and punched the Prince in the face. The elf staggered back. Tyric said, "You should know your father sent me on a mission to find an artifact at Emperor's Keep." Tyric punched the Prince again.

"He has been mad too long; you cannot believe anything he says. Stories he tells children. Just stories. " Prince Elraf brought his sword tip up trying to protect himself from the foe he could not see.

Tyric spun the handle of his ax so the tips of the twin blades locked the elf's sword. Tyric snapped his hand back and wrenched the sword from the Prince. On his back swing, he saw a guard curling around the trees with his sword raised. Tyric turned, letting his ax continue, he cut through the leg of the guard. The elf fell screaming and frantic to staunch the flow of blood rushing from his leg. Tyric turned and Prince Elraf had cleared his eyes and reached for his sword. Tyric took three steps and stepped on Prince Elraf's sword binding it to the ground. Tyric's fist whirled around and caught the Prince in the face again. His fist lifted the elf off his feet and spun him to land on his shoulder blades, his feet flipping over him and laying him out flat on the ground. Tyric leaped passed him, seeing the Prince wiggle his hands like a surprised turtle trying to right itself. Tyric ran into the forest knowing the guards would need to attend their leader before they could consider pursuit.

Prince Elraf rolled over, drew a deep breath, and yelled, "Perhaps you are right, blacksmith. The Egg will save the World. Or madness!" He laughed.

Chapter XV: Cliff of Thieves

Tyric flitted through the woods, the crossbow bolts landed wild of him slipping under the leaves to the sides, sinking into the tree trunks high and low, and a few arcing out of sight with no apparent landing. Then the fletching of a longbow arrow whisked passed his ear and buried itself into the coarse bark of a walnut trunk six feet across. Even at this range, Tyric knew the hit from that type of bow could be deadly. He put the walnut between him and the bow. Then another beech tree. A maple and several cherry trees. The trees here stood so large and the space between them so wide that it reminded Tyric of a cathedral. He paused and listened in this empty church with the long dark ceiling high above.

No sounds came to him.

His mind raced to calculate his distance with that longbow shot, the direction he had taken in the wood, and Anika's path. He memorized the trees here in case he needed to backtrack. He holstered his ax and sprinted to intersect Anika's path ahead. He hoped she had not veered from her course.

Tyric's boot sunk into sucking mud. He saw where Anika's prints took her through the edge of this same marsh. Found a dry rock and rested. His breath ragged and his armor hot. He looked at her prints. One foot seemed to drag every few steps as if she limped. *Had the Prince's guards struck her with an arrow?* He leaped from the rock and ran forward.

The ground dried as he went up hill and her prints became less easy to follow. She moved fast but he could see the wound slowed her pace. In a damp ravine, he found a swipe of blood on the edge of a fern. He growled, "I see they did wound you. You'll be slower. Maybe I will catch you." *Why am I also concerned for you?*

Ahead Tyric heard a woman's scream – Anika's scream. Tyric sprinted through the trees. The brush multiplied and he knew he neared a clearing. He heard voices including Anika's but too low and far yet. He pushed through the brush ignoring the scratching thorns and eased against the clearing, staying behind a tall hickory commanding its own post.

The clearing opened like a wedge, the far side showed a cliff with a long drop. Anika stood with her back to the cliff, surrounded by the same rough scrabble of desperate men he remembered ringed him around the forge fire tree and then again at the castle, six of them.

" … Tyric. Where is the blacksmith?"

"… killed … wizard …" Anika said. He watched her lips move but even though Tyric strained his ears and held his breath, the wind blew her words away.

" … He escaped Prince Frael … we are impatient … give us …"

"No!" Anika said.

Tyric took his ax in hand. He saw half the assassins wore wrist mounted mini crossbows and had them pointed at Anika. Her leg showed a broken off longbow arrow in the back of her thigh that she favored. Tyric looked around and saw he had chosen his approach poorly. Another copse of trees to his far left would have provided better cover and be closer. It would take too long to move around.

One of the assassins lifted his sword and strode toward Anika. He held the blade tip near her throat. Tyric saw her stand unmoving, "Kill me and you ... never get ... egg."

"I think we will find ... just fine."

"I'll fall ... what will happen?"

Tyric burst from behind the tree. He covered half the distance to the assassins before the first of them turned. Tyric used his ax to shield himself from the first crossbow bolt. The second crossbow bolt he batted from the air with his ax and it flew wide. The third crossbow bolt he backhanded against the face of his ax and the dart returned at its sender. The bolt ripped through his leather armor collar and into his throat. The assassin fell clawing at the arrow but his motions weakened as Tyric came amongst them. He looked for one marked like a wizard but he saw none. His ax flailed against their bodies. Another fell before their swords came up to block his swing. He spun his ax head and yanked the first sword away. The assassin pulled a pair of daggers from his belt and lurched at Tyric. Tyric kicked the legs from under the assassin, arched his back and tumbled the man to the ground. His ax came around and split the ribs of the next nearest assassin. Tyric felt the scratch of daggers against his back plate. He kicked back and heard the air rush out of his attacker and thump to the ground. Tyric's ax cleaved up and split the next one from his chin to his cranium.

"Not so fast, Tyric," said the assassin at the cliff with Anika.

Tyric tipped his helmet down at seeing one of the wounded assassins next to him reaching shaking fingers for a long dagger. Tyric stomped his heel onto the fingers with a rippling crunch.

Tyric strode toward the two at the edge of the cliff.

The assassin said, "Don't come any closer."

"I wanted to make sure you heard me when I said go ahead. She means nothing to me. She stole from me. However, you'll still need to kill me and you will have lost something you wanted."

The assassin's sword wavered.

Tyric heard movement behind him, "Stay there a minute." He walked back to the assassin that crawled at him with a dagger in his teeth desperately cocking a crossbow in spite of his broken fingers. "I know your mission will keep you from ever stopping." Tyric stabbed the assassin with the tip of his ax. Tyric returned to the assassin threatening Anika. "And I am unsafe until you are all dead. So help me understand how you threatening her, will save you?"

"If she dies you will not have the egg she carries either."

"Have you seen that egg?"

"No."

"It's not from a chicken. It's durable. It can take more abuse than falling off a cliff. Why do you think no one ever opened it in a thousand years?"

The assassin swallowed, the leather helmet he wore looked to be sliding off his smooth head under the sweat that beaded it. He turned his sword to menace Tyric.

Tyric measured the paces to the assassin. He dashed at the man and jumped. The assassin braced for an ax strike from Tyric's overhead hold of his ax. Tyric landed at an angle like sliding into a child's game he remembered from when he was young. His moving weight mounded up the dirt and rocks and tore at the sod. The dirt rolled like a carpet under the assassin, a carpet that flew over the edge of the cliff.

Tyric twisted his body, dug his fingers into the sod further back, and stopped his own slide. He pushed up to his knees and stood. His ax dangled from his fingers as he approached Anika. "How do I trust you?"

She stepped away from the edge of the cliff, "You can't."

"Why did you steal the egg?"

"My mission," she took another step toward the forest. "The mission doesn't seem so important now."

"Is that so?"

"Yes."

"Are you on any other missions? Like these assassins?"

"No. Not anymore."

"Again, how do I trust you? I don't see how I can ever believe you." Tyric holstered his ax.

"You can't, but I can promise and keep to that promise."

"You have training beyond any I've seen. Beyond this crew sent after us. I probably only needed to save you because the Prince's guard flagged you with that arrow. How reliable is the promise of an assassin? One staying close to King Ek, infiltrating, scheming, and planning? A weapon hidden just like those daggers rolled up in the map that day."

"I protected the King. I stopped the assassin dressed as a cook from giving the King poison."

"A good story. You carried a similar vial of poison."

"As good a story as the one where you killed the assassins and now range hunted for murder."

"What was, or is, your mission?"

"You."

"*I* was your mission?"

"I have to sit down," Anika hobbled to a nearby rock and sat down keeping her wounded leg straight. "War is coming." She plucked a blade of grass and studied the broken end. "I was to seduce you at the castle when you came to repair the King's armor. The other fools pushed their plan ahead attempting to kill the King, ordered by Prince Frael."

"But not the same as hired you?"

"No. Different branch of the Rubied Assassins." She sighed, "The right hand doesn't know what the left hand is doing."

Tyric said, "Can't trust an assassin."

"None of that is important. You don't know who you are. The words written at Emperor's Keep are about you. You are one of the six."

"Those words said two of them die. I don't want to

be part of that."

"What do you remember of your childhood? Always an orphan?"

Tyric nodded, "I remember Erolok telling me I was alone when I was a skinny kid of seven, that he would teach me a trade to be proud of. I don't remember anything before then."

"I thought so," she looked up at him, "They sent me to kill you."

"Sent to kill me?"

Anika nodded. "I saw you up close. I saw who you are. The two Princes have been keeping back from their father because they both understood the general truths about the Dragon's Egg and they wanted it for themselves. The King kept it from them, not trusting either but when knowing his situation was faltering he gave the secret to you."

"Because he knows my link to those words?"

"No. Because you saved him and the war is coming. He chose you. I've seen why. Breaking one's mission is not a light choice. The Rubied Assassins will hunt me until I die. You have my promise that I am done with the mission."

"How reliable is the promise of an assassin?"

"None. But I'm telling you –"

Tyric waved his arm, "No talisman or oath to speak that binds even an assassin?"

"No. Just my word."

"And how good is that word?" Tyric dropped his arms.

"Very. My word kept me on my missions."

He pointed at her, "Like this mission you are aborting?"

A slight smile pulled at the corners of Anika's mouth, "Ah, yes."

Tyric folded his arms across his chest, "So how do I trust you?"

Anika asked, "Why did you rescue me?"

"I found I worried about you."

"Worrying about the egg I carried?"

"No, about you –"

"Why is that?" Anika wrinkled her nose as she smiled.

Tyric put his hand out for her. She gripped his fingers and he pulled her to her feet, "I guess I liked having you with me." He drew her close and pressed his lips to hers. She melted into his arms and returned his kiss.

Chapter XVI: Kolomis

Prince Frael pushed through the tangling vines that ringed the clearing, itself filled with rank thistles. The giant vulture sat in the top of an old oak and swiveled its bald, flame-colored head around at his approach. Its bumpy mottled skin exposed pin feather tufts and straggling hairs that enhanced its appearance as a maggot infested corpse. The bird snapped its hooked beak and watched him with its sharp glassy eyes. The bird ruffled its jet black feathers and smoothed out its black leathery wings, which spanned wider than the tree's canopy before it folded them along its greasy back. It turned around on the thick oak branch it perched on revealing talons that stretched longer and sharper than freshly made swords. Tether ropes dripped to the ground not far from a large boulder that Kolomis sat on.

Kolomis sat with his legs crossed and his head bowed in meditation. Prince Frael evaluated the plate armor that covered Kolomis' body. His hands passed his wrists and up his forearms were shielded by spiked and armored gauntlets. Plate armor shingled down his body to his knees where his leg armor finished inside tall solid boots. The black armor glinted sharp in the noon sun while angry volcanic runes shimmered across the larger plates a thousand years old. The armor showed heavy battle marks and Kolomis' black dragon cloak was missing. The heat of the day? Some other reason? Two long swords splayed at his side, their grips canted forward and ready for anything, the space between filled with a picket fence of dagger hilts.

Kolomis had heard the vulture rustling and opened his eyes. He tilted his head. A grin splayed his dark lips that pulled back over black tushes, "Punctual as usual."

"Yes."

"I somehow guess you will tell me the Rubied Assassins have failed us, again."

"Yes, sir. Tyric still eludes them." Prince Frael held up the stump of his wrist, "This is what I lost in personally trying to capture him. He killed my dragon cloak."

"I don't know how those Rubied Assassins have any kind of reputation besides a bad one." He tilted his head and pursed his dark lips that bulged around his black tushes. "Their limited success in destroying the siblings is maddening and unfortunate." Kolomis sighed. Prince Frael somehow felt more fear upon hearing that sigh than a burst of anger filled screaming by any other. Kolomis swung his feet around and slid off the rock. He pushed aside thistles and walked closer to Prince Frael. "I want the Rubied Assassins retrained."

"We have been training them thoroughly –"

"And yet they fail, again." Kolomis walked around Prince Frael, scanning his robes. "The Rubied Assassins were a great resource for the Shadow Wizard in the Old War. He will be disappointed with us."

"Their existence and support kept secret by members of the Enkarian Elf family, at least by those that did not have Rule."

"A distraction for the non-ruling family members. Run in secret. Yes, I know." Kolomis tapped his fingertip on the plate covering his thigh. The thud-thud-thud like a dangerous heartbeat or the latching of the retention mechanism of a catapult. "I think we may need to use the Shadow Wizard's Crimson Knights."

"Who are the Crimson Knights?" Prince Frael heard his own voice filled with more fear than he wanted to reveal.

"You don't want to meet them. They are the Shadow Wizard's guard. Wizard warriors. A new creation of his since the Old War. I fear nothing and they give me pause. Violent, unpredictable, tough, and rapacious. The Shadow Wizard will send them to visit us and complete the tasks we have been unable to finish."

Prince Frael swallowed the words. "Are ... are there many of these knights?"

"I don't know how it matters. One is unstoppable. I saw it spar with other creatures the Shadow Wizard has found or created and it killed them all. So I don't know. The Shadow Wizard learned from his last defeat. He ensures nothing stops his control of the land this time. He has toiled diligently for the last thousand years, motivated by unfettered anger and revenge."

Prince Frael brushed his fingers through his hair, nervous jitters loosening more hairs than his attempt at resetting them hoped to effect.

Kolomis asked, "Are you King, yet?"

"My father is dead. I rule the Enkarian Elves now. Yes, I am King."

"Have you started the elves making weapons?"

"Not yet. But they will soon."

"I will send you more korlak and the Shadow Staff we promised you." Kolomis turned and walked toward the giant vulture.

Prince Frael objected, "I don't need korlak. Nor did I bargain for them. Just the staff."

"No. You will take the korlak as promised. Concern yourself with killing Tyric and reclaiming the egg. If you must make a choice, kill Tyric over saving the egg. He is more dangerous to our plans."

"Yes."

Prince Frael watched Kolomis mount the giant bird. The trunk of the old oak shuddered and swayed as the monstrous creature crouched low and sprang into the air. His eyes tracked the bird as it flew west. He knew Kolomis went to meet with the Shadow Wizard. The prince hoped news of his failures might escape the discussion, or at least be only a small footnote.

Chapter XVII: Dragon Climb

Tyric heard, "Tyric, wake up, you're having a dream!" Anika shook his shoulder.

He rolled over and sat up. The fire burned in smokeless embers and glowed red like the eyes he had seen in the vision fading from his mind. He rubbed his face remembering important pieces of the dream as the images faded.

Anika knelt next to him, "What was it?"

Glad that she remained, with the egg, and he was alive. Maybe his trust in her held stronger than he feared. "The Elf King. He came to me from the forest."

"What did he say?"

"We have to search for a cave. The cave is between the middle peaks of Dragon Tooth range."

Anika said, "There are six mountains that make up the Teeth."

"You are familiar with them? I have not been that far East of the castle."

"I trained climbing south of that range but we used them as a marker. They warned us not to climb in that range. Probably because of the dragon."

"He said a dragon's fire is needed to roast it open. Just like the pine tree that has seeds that only open after a forest fire. Then you woke me. I hope that is all he needed to tell us."

"How do we avoid getting eaten by the dragon?"

"That. That is what I worry he might have told me and I didn't hear it because you woke me." Tyric shook off the blanket and rolled it up. He kicked a few sticks into the embers and they flamed up. "Eat more of the assassin's food and then we will continue."

"I shot that rabbit over there with the wrist bow before you made all the noise. I saw it in the glow of the moon."

Tyric nodded, seeing the rabbit already skinned and spitted, "Looks good for breakfast." He was relieved she had not shot him with the crossbow. He tried staying awake but the running, the fighting, and the chasing had added too much fatigue. He knew he had to sleep eventually and not have a choice but to trust Anika. Neither of them said anything of the kiss since they stood by the cliff. The smell of her that close to him, a week ago now, seemed a stronger memory than the dream message from the King minutes earlier. "How is your leg?"

"The bandages hold the wound tight enough it feels ok. It will heal. Thanks."

Tyric nodded, "Best if we cut straight east from here and follow the Zytakar mountains north."

"Since the mountains curve so much northeast it will make it easier to find the Dragon Tooth peaks."

* * *

The ground went down into swamps that followed the edge of the mountains. Eventually the rain that dropped over the forest and against the mountain slopes found its way to the Lakes of Tadur and eventually all the way south to Kytran Bay. Here though, against the hard mountains pressed by the forest, the water pooled in brackish pits tinged with boot sucking mud.

"Think any fords exist across this swamp?"

"No evidence yet." Anika pulled a foot out of the mud and splashed it down for her next step.

"This is tiring." Tyric took another step and his foot felt like the mud had no bottom. "No, we go more west, it's getting deeper again." Mud streaked up and down the pole he prodded ahead with as well as smeared up his leg armor where he had stepped into a hole deeper than expected. "There is snow in the mountains."

"Are you asking a question or just telling me? We just look up there and see the snow."

"We will need snowshoes." Tyric moved to a fallen tree, swung his leg up, and twisted around to sit. "Have you used snowshoes before?"

"A few times."

"I haven't. They are not something people regularly ask a blacksmith to make for them. We could make them for the snow since we have plenty of materials here and use them to cross the swamp as easy as the snow later."

Anika pulled herself onto the log but Tyric already stood on it and walked down the length. He hacked vines with his dagger and split wood off with his ax.

Tyric returned and sat down, "You've made rope before?"

"No."

"Take these vines and hammer them until the fibers release, then bunch them like this and twist them together. See?"

Anika nodded. She took the vines and hammered on them with the pommel-nut of her dagger. Tyric split the wood with his knife and bent it around into hoops. Then he made rope himself. "Take your boot off." Tyric pulled his off and set it on the log next to him. He tugged at his sock and stuffed it in his boot. "Fresh air for little toes."

Anika giggled. "Now that I can wiggle my toes, what should I do?"

"Take the end of the rope you've started and hold it with your toes. That frees up your hands to twist and add more fibers."

"Oh, I see." After a time she said, "This is nice, doing this."

"That's because you're a natural at it. My rope is too coarse."

"But it's thicker. How much do we need?"

"I remember the cord crosses both ways like a fishing net, which takes a lot. Bigger hoops will support more weight. We get up on the mountain snow above the tree line and we can't repair them, so testing down here will help us later."

Anika paused and listened, putting her hand out to quiet Tyric. She glanced around, her ears searched for the rustling she heard from a mouse or a squirrel. Tyric looked up and saw the approaching coils of a swamp python droop down toward Anika. "That's the biggest snake I've ever seen." Tyric dropped the rope he worked on and it rolled off the log and hooked in the tips of the grass below. He released his ax.

Anika followed his eyes and saw the snake directly over her head. She rolled along the log and pulled her sword as she stood. The snake halted. Its glassy eyes thinking while its head bobbed from side to side as it watched them. A flicking tongue tasted the air. She saw along the log that another huge snake slithered up the tree trunk intent on Tyric. "Look out!"

Tyric swung his ax and the snake's head tumbled free of the body. The length of the snake whipped around and dropped to the swamp with a splash. Tyric reached for his boot and stuffed his foot into it.

"I can't reach it yet." Anika held her sword before her. "It's wondering what to do now." Tyric holstered his ax and undid some of the extra rope they scavenged from the assassins. He made a loop and tossed it into the air around the snake. Tyric tugged the rope and it tightened around the snake. The snake pulled up to disappear into the trees overhead. Tyric forced it down. "Get your boot on and collect our things. Look to your left and behind you." Tyric let the snake have more rope while he straddled the tree trunk to grip it like riding a horse. He pulled on the rope and stretched the snake closer to them. His arms bulged as the snake tugged back. Anika plucked the cords and hoops from the grass tips where they fell and stuffed all of it in her pack. "I see more snakes coming this way. Swamp rattlers and black bottle snakes plus more pythons."

Tyric grunted, pulling against the snake, "I've never seen swamp pythons this far north. Ready?"

"Yes."

Tyric pulled hard on the rope. On the snake's rebound, he snapped his ax around and cut the end from the rope. The snake whipped itself back up into the tree and uncoiled a few loops trying to balance, squeezing the limb from which it suspended. It did not fall.

They ran along the trunk of the tree and leaped into the swamp. They hurried as fast as the muck allowed. They slashed at the faster snakes and ensured they killed the most dangerous.

Anika sliced at a black bottle snake, cutting its head off, "I've never seen so many snakes."

"Nor I," Tyric put a hand in a leafy bush to help him pull his feet forward while he hacked at a rattlesnake. "Is Prince Frael nearby?"

"I haven't seen anyone but us and these snakes." Anika stabbed and killed another serpent.

A python dropped down from the vines hanging over Tyric. Tyric turned and sliced a long length of the snake off with his ax. He stepped back and felt no bottom to the mud hole. Chest deep in the muck he yelled, "Quicksand!" He twisted his head to see Anika. She thrashed against three vipers that hissed and struck at her. She was already down to her hips, "Me too!" The vipers came close enough that she sliced through all of them with one swing. Their loss immaterial since the underbrush seethed with too many replacements.

Tyric looked for sticks or vines and nothing was nearby that he could put his fingers on, "Anika, can you reach my fingers?" She stretched, her fingertips touching his, and then he had her hand. "I see better ground to the far side of us. I'm going to pull you to me and throw you over there. You give me a rope and tie it to something."

"You'll go down with my extra weight while tossing me."

"Then give me the end of your rope and tie it to my wrist."

Anika wiggled the rope off her waist and tied it around his arm, sliding it down over his wrist. She pulled it tight. The other end of the rope she tied to her own wrist. Snakes slithered across the muck. Anika slashed at them with her sword. Tyric coiled his muscles and pulled her to him slow at first as she slipped from the sucking mud and then fast as she skipped across the surface. Tyric dipped deeper in the mud, lapping against his arm and slowing his throw. He kicked his feet and completed his throw. Anika landed on the mud but rolled before it gripped her. The rocky soil held firm against her body when she sprang to her feet and ran the rope around a tree root that arched over a wet hole like the talon of a beast scratching at the soil. She looked back as she tied the rope and saw only Tyric's fist gripping the slack rope and a dozen snakes spiraling around him. She tugged on the rope and he pulled. The mud and his armor protected him from the snakebites until he could swing his ax and kill them. He gripped the rope anew and pulled. He crawled ashore and stood. Anika killed another leading snake. "Hopefully, this is more than an island." He swung his ax and cut the knot Anika tied the rope with, "We'll need the rope, no time to untie it." He coiled the rope as they ran forward into the brush. Then the brush opened and they moved upward on sloping, drying land.

Tyric said, "I think we made it to a spur of the mountains. We can move fast enough to outrun the snakes now."

"I don't know how much more swamp I could endure," Anika said. She saw the snakes stayed in the swamp and refused to follow them into the dryer scrub.

They hurried up the first of many hills that rippled like the muscles of the world into the taller peaks. The mud dried on their bodies and fell off in cracked chunks or was scrubbed from them by the dense brush. Tyric banged the mud-caked ropes against tree trunks lightening them and returning their suppleness as they walked. He slapped mud off Anika's pack with the end of the rope releasing a cloud of dusty mud chips. He slapped her bottom.

"Hey!" she turned to him.

He grinned, "You had muck on your back."

"That wasn't my back."

Tyric's arm looped around her and he kissed her. When he broke away he said, "I shouldn't have done that. It was for saving me, though."

She leaned closer to him, "Did I indicate you should stop?" She kissed him and they lingered, her fingers at the side of his dusty face. When she pulled back she said, "Think a wizard caused all the snakes to chase us?"

"Yes. Who is back there? We should go."

"Should we talk about the kissing?" Anika tipped her head to the side.

"Yes. But more talk when we get to a safer place," Tyric knew it might be some time yet.

The hills bent upward into rocky climbs. The trees thinned and the temperatures dropped. They slept huddled on a narrow shelf with their blankets tight, foregoing some of the padding around the dragon's egg, but they cradled the egg between them and used its warmth.

Tyric said, "I worried the egg might freeze when we got to higher elevations."

Anika touched her fingers to it, "I'm glad it stays so warm."

The wind pressed their backs and swirled around their heads. They climbed with ropes and pitons now. Their movement slowed.

Tyric shouted as he dangled by one hand, "We charged up the first mountain we saw, should we have gone further north?"

"The whole range is like this, nothing easy here. The snakes may have pushed us toward an easier path than others we could take further north."

"Good thing you've done this before."

"You have an eye for the stone and the equipment."

"I made some of these for a few people traveling through, I guess they needed them."

"How many did you make?" Anika sunk the next piton into the wall.

"They needed a lot. I can't remember exactly. Took me a week. These were the less pretty ones."

"We're climbing with your rejected equipment?"

"It's all functional, just not pretty."

"That was probably for the same time I trained. Enough equipment for a large group with a specific travel need."

Tyric pulled himself up, "Yes. I guess." He cinched his rope while he moved one of the other pitons, tapping it into place. "I see another ledge up there."

Anika looked along the face of the rock. Below, fog settled across the tree tops, floating among them like specters on the hunt. Above she saw the sharp edge Tyric indicated. The ledge went both ways along the mountain side until the distance blurred the edge into the regular mountain textures. "I had forgotten about the first step of the giants."

"First step?"

"That ledge is wider than it appears from here. It cuts along the whole range. Like a road but this high up with no ramp at the ends. We can go from here to the base of the Dragon Teeth and then on from there to the next step."

"More ledges?"

"Giant steps apart."

Tyric climbed higher, "I see how a dragon can stay safe up here. No easy way."

Anika eased her body over the edge of the sharp rock rimming the giant step. She rolled closer to the mountain and away from the edge. Tyric swung his body over the edge and joined her laying on the hard flat rock. Striations ran along the end of the rock as if it poured from an ancient volcano and ran along this trench before the mountains rose up or the land of the swamp fell down. Bird nests spun from grass waved with discarded feathers out of crevasses between the mountain and scabby piles of accumulated loose rock that fell from above. He saw how the smoothness of the step showed knocks where boulders had tumbled down the mountain and struck the edge away.

Tyric commented, "The smoothness of the ledge hides its danger. All that gravel makes the place as slippery as dried peas on a plate."

Anika nodded, "A risk, certainly."

Tyric stood and scuffed his foot. The pebbles and rocks scattered, many of them rolling off the edge of the shelf into the silent forest and fog below. Tyric settled his pack with a shrug of his shoulder and walked north. Anika rolled over and watched him for a dozen steps before pushing to her feet and catching him.

The fog dispersed ahead of a bitter wind filled with rain. The temperature plummeted like the rocks Tyric still kicked out from his feet before stepping forward. The sharp winds crackled across the ledge driving particles of sleet against their bodies as if it were sand.

Tyric pulled his cowl up close around his ears. The snow chattered against their blankets that had crusted into a crackly carapace and remained the only sound besides the shrieking winds. Tyric felt the heat of the egg against his back.

Anika pulled down the top of her blanket with chilled fingers. "Tyric," she shouted. The brisk winds stretched out her words in thin harsh wires, "This doesn't feel right. Something is wrong."

Tyric said, "Yes, something out there." He scanned the misty swirl of ice pellets beyond the edge of the shelf. Darkness shuffled about them and transformed the mid-day sun with their ominous shadows. "I worry about this ice."

Anika shivered, "Me too." She scanned the frigid mountain for shelter but saw only unyielding stone.

The snap of violet lightning reached for them from the void beyond the ledge. The electric power surged against the rocky wall blasting the stone into showering crystals that burned with sulfur. Another lance of purple struck from above, carving black lines across the wall and before their path. A third and a fourth blast sought them.

A giant vulture appeared out of the storm, wheeling in the air. The shadows cast from its wings caused ancient instincts in Tyric and Anika to cower against the mountain. The vulture released heavy boulders from its talons that smacked the mountain and bounced over the cliff edge.

Tyric said, "What weapons do we have for this?"

"Nothing." Anika watched the vulture bank for another attack. "This small crossbow will do nothing."

"We are too exposed here. We need to move."

Purple lightning struck Tyric in vicious, burning pain. He floated in a purple cloud. The rock, hard and cold, pushed against his forehead. He put a hand up to push away the icy rock. Its coldness hurt his thoughts. Tyric moaned as his hand burned a fever through his body. The fire in his hand came from his ring. He reached for the band holding his gem, he would discard it, fling it from the cliff. Then a less pained part of his mind took control. He concentrated. Blue sparks sliced across the blackening purple haze. His thoughts swept through the gem in jagged and unsteady lines of power. He regained control. He envisioned a crystal ax whirling though his gem, slicing the violet streaks and stabbing at the darkness. A deafening crack roared from the sky, striking Tyric's body. His arms squirmed in anguish, his teeth shot out beams of pain, but his mind remained calm. Tyric's thoughts swung his ax and struck into the heart of the gem where the violet seemed the darkest. Dark and light swirled in madness about his mind. Buffeting black wings. He heard Anika scream. His ax rose against the purple fog and he struck it. The violet power ran red with blood and the power faded. Tyric sensed his body still lay on the ledge and he pushed up. The buffeting winds spun around him.

The vulture gripped the edge of the ledge with one talon while the other snagged Anika's blanket. The vulture scratched her toward the edge of the abyss. A wizard rode atop the vulture and swung a staff in the air. Tyric saw a coalescing purple fog gather about the wizard. Tyric picked up the end of one of their ropes that had fallen off his pack. He wrapped it in a cross around the head of his ax and twisted the free end about his other hand. He sprinted toward the vulture. His first swing chopped through the toe of the talon that tugged at Anika. His second swing he released the ax to fly through the air to spear through the wizard's torso. The wizard's magic exploded. The wizard slumped in his saddle. The back of the vulture crackled and burst open with purple arcs. The bird's wings stopped beating and it fell back in a greasy smudge toward the forest top. Tyric pulled on his rope and the ax wedged around the saddle horn. He watched the rope chase the bird down.

"Don't let go of that rope," Anika ran toward the edge, "But hold the end of this one." She dove from the edge into the air. The vulture's wings fluttered and slowed its fall. Anika caught it, freed the ax and gripped the rope. Her rope yanked her and she slammed against the wall. Tyric's feet slid on the loose rocks and bits of fractured ice covering the ledge. He dropped to his hip and kicked his feet against the ground. He wrapped Anika's rope around his forearm and reached for his belt. His dagger had fallen out of his belt and lay behind him. The edge of the mountain neared and a few rock chips kicked by his feet already launched off the lip and into the void. Tyric shoved his hand into his belt pouch and pulled out his dinner fork. He twisted over and stabbed the fork into the stone. The tines bent and scraped across the ledge. One foot hit the air. He spun the fork in his fingers and slammed the pick-like handle into a pocket notched by some ancient falling rock off the top of the mountain. His slide stopped. He pulled himself back onto the ledge and put his knee behind the fork. It bent at an alarming angle but Tyric wiggled out of his pack and gripped a climbing spike. He wedged that in there and tied off the ropes.

"Hey, what's going on up there?" Anika asked.

"We're lucky." Tyric hammered in another spike closer to the mountain in a better fissure. He put his boot to this spike and pulled the ropes up. When Anika crawled onto the ledge Tyric said, "An insane action."

"I've seen what you do with that ax. We will need it."

The sky pulsated in a swirling mix of deep violet and vile blackness.

Anika said, "I thought you killed the wizard."

"There must be another –" Tyric fell to his knees when an arc of lightning curling out of the storm struck him. A song someone sang when he was young wiggled out of his mind amid the pain. *Know the purple fingers, lancing through the sky; seek safety 'fore the storm, 'ere you wither and die.*

The sky rumbled, readying to belch forth another shock of splintering power.

Tyric wriggled for the wall on his belly. Maybe the rocks and the bird nests could protect him.

He heard Anika's voice small and far away ask, "Are you all right?"

He shook his head and continued crawling. Why did his gem not protect him from this obvious wizardry? Was it much too powerful or a different magic? Or did his ring fail? His mind wandered into his gem. He found power there like a shell on a sandy beach. He picked it up and looked at it, flipping the light shell between his fingers. The shell fragmented into slivers of steel that wove into a hard wall that covered both of them. It dug into the rock above and scooped into the rock below. The lightning struck against the wall like rain against a metal roof – a thick metal slab of a roof.

"What is it?" Anika asked next to his ear.

"Me." Tyric stirred with his voice. He pushed to his knees, turned, and sat with his back to the stone wall. They listened to the sleet and the lightning.

"The wizard will be here."

"That's what I expect."

"How will we kill him? Can we escape from this?" Anika touched the shield, cold and hard.

"I can remove it. I think." Tyric closed his eyes and put his thoughts into his gem again. The iron slab flexed, then lifted away, dripping bits of stone that clung to it. Tyric opened his eyes and watched the slab float between them and the purple lightning.

"How are you doing that?"

"Through my gem." Tyric glanced at his hand. The blue of the gem was the deepest shade he had seen in it. "Through me." The lightning continued searching for them, but the iron slab hung there. Tyric waved his hand and the slab spun like a carriage wheel. "We still need to go up, right?"

Anika looked from the lightning to the shield that protected them to Tyric, "Yes."

"Then we should climb again. It's easy to control this. Come closer to me." Anika came near Tyric. He took her hand in his and put his arm around her, holding her tight. The iron shield slammed around them adhering to the rock again. "Like a turtle we have a shell. Let's climb." He felt Anika nod.

They climbed with the constant sound of lightning striking their shield. The noise droned into the background of the wind. Eventually the lightning stopped coming from the clouds. "Must have gotten bored or tired."

Anika said, "Or waiting?"

"Possible."

"What can you do with the shield?"

Tyric closed his eyes and the shield thinned and shrunk down until it was the size of a coin. Then it shrunk to the size of a grain of sand and vanished. They continued climbing. They rested on the second giant's step and then again on the third step. The cliff face became softer and more dangerous as they climbed with the freeze and thaw cycles that happened at this elevation. They slowed down and ensured their gear gripped living stone.

The cliffs ended at the fourth ledge. A climb faced them of scrabble, not ropes and pitons. Still steep and slow. The cold dropped so that snow and ice remained constant on the hard rocks.

Tyric asked, "What do you remember ahead?"

"We only climbed to the second giant step. This is all new here."

Tyric took another step, "What other training have you had?"

Anika said, "The Rubied Assassins get a lot. I had most. You've seen the core skills."

"Combat, travel through inhospitable lands, climbing."

"– Blending into a crowd, playing a role for years

to get good placement."

Tyric paused, "What about ... love?"

"Some missions require it."

"What did you think about it?"

"No different than killing. When it's necessary." Anika met Tyric's eyes, "You're not making judgments?"

"No."

"Rubied Assassins are too expensive to hire to eliminate your average fat shopkeeper. Not until a target gathers wealth and extreme power do others want to take it away. So working into their organization and their life can be exciting."

"So have you? ..."

"When you are in the Rubied Assassins you are a weapon. Love is a minor sin to break when your goal is killing."

"You seem like you enjoyed all aspects of it."

Anika's eyes flared, "You're there to kill them."

"What missions have you had?"

"I never had that kind of mission."

Tyric said, "That's much better, you only kill."

"Hey," Anika pulled at Tyric's arm. "You asked me what training I had –"

"– and what can I believe? You said they sent you to kill me. Is that still your plan?"

"What do you think? I could have let you drown in that quicksand while those snakes bit your wrist. Or many days before or since. When I chased off that cliff to save your weapon."

"That was foolish to chase my ax. Why didn't you kill me?"

Anika said, "The danger of being more than an assassin is –"

"A failed assassin?"

"You want me to change my mind about you?" Anika said, "It's easy with the training and the life I have had – to remain objective and distance my emotions from ... you."

Tyric pulled himself forward up the mountain, "What can I trust?"

Anika put her hands to her forehead, pushing her hair back, her voice elevating, "How do I convince you? Two things –" Anika crunched through the snow crawling to Tyric. She pulled his face to hers – and kissed him. She spread his fingers and pressed his hand against her heart. "Feel that?"

Tyric nodded.

"Every step we take that beat becomes more yours." Anika turned away. "Even if that is not enough ..." She looked over the vast forest far below them.

Tyric took his hand back, "It's the murder of the King's advisors. They think I did that so they pursue me. Now this egg. Not you. You would be safe away from me."

"The Rubied Assassins and all their allies are hunting me for getting too involved with you – actively helping you. A rule among the guild. I am in as much danger as you. I will never be safe. Then I saw the words on the wall of the egg chamber. We were supposed to find the words. Either the Elf King put them there or someone close to the real legend did."

"You're getting carried away. The simplest reason is why we are pursued."

Anika pulled at Tyric's collar, "The magic our enemies are putting against us is old."

"How do you know magic, are you a wizard too?"

"No." Anika pushed Tyric back, "The Rubied Assassins are taught to recognize magic by those friendly with the guild. I studied with Carmela at Levet Fortress and an important tapestry hangs there. I didn't realize it at the time." Anika closed her eyes against the sharp cutting wind. "A fabulous piece of work. The tapestry depicts King Aleron's coronation in the great hall at Emperor's Keep."

Tyric strapped on his snowshoes.

Anika paused and put her snowshoes on. "The first coronation since the beginning of the third age, immediately after Aleron defeated the Kelvin Mage's forces from the southern swamps. Aleron had risen from the ranks of a lieutenant in the dwindling human armies to commander of their victories. The people hailed him as King."

Tyric stomped his feet to ensure the bindings remained tight. "Then the Shadow Wizard led the hordes of korlak against both the humans and the kelvin. Those attacks forced Aleron and the Kelvin Mage to unite their bitter armies against their common foe. The Shadow Wizard destroyed Aleron and Emperor's Keep, but the Shadow Wizard perished when the walls fell."

"Carmella told me the Shadow Wizard remained

very much alive. I'm not sure how she knows that."

Tyric put a foot forward into the snow. He took a second step, "And so we have the Shadow Wizard chasing us."

"Or someone found his magic."

"Perhaps someone wants everyone to think the Shadow Wizard is behind them?"

"Imagine if it *is* the Shadow Wizard? A wizard with more than one lifespan to prepare? What could you do with small pebbles through time? How big could the plans get? How wide your powers? Why did that lightning hurt you when other magic has not?" Anika balled a fistful of snow and threw it across the mountain where Tyric could easily see it even though he had his back to her as he climbed. The snowball arced around as it hit the snow, sticking clumps of snow to itself. It grew. The weight of the new snow turned it faster and pressed more snow to it. Small rocks stuck in the great wheel as it wobbled down the side of the mountain and launched off the edge of the fourth giant step. They watched the snow wheel disappear into the forest, flattening the far away trees.

"Don't fall down." Tyric said over his shoulder.

Anika climbed next to Tyric. They did not speak between the measured steps up the side of the mountain, their snowshoes keeping them atop the drifts. The wind curled sideway around splintered fists of stone like pieces from the giant that used the steps. The wind gathered and blew loose ice and grit at them. A growl snatched across the snow from behind a jumble of rocks. A great white cat stalked toward them.

"Tyric!" Anika said, pointing with a finger while retrieving her sword with her other. Across from the blacksmith the powerful telnak – the snow cat – paced, swinging its gaze from Anika to Tyric.

"Of course, cats as large as the dogs chase us too," Tyric's ax spun in his hands. A low feline growl rumbled from its body, the thunder crackling in their chests. Anika balanced her sword in the air before her, slicing and cutting to draw the cat's gaze from Tyric. The cat's ears flicked at Anika's faster heart rate but its eyes remained locked on Tyric. It moved slowly closer as it paced. Then it raised a back ripping snarl as it sprang at Tyric. Tyric lashed with his ax as he twirled away from the rushing creature, drawing a searing red line across its white fur.

The telnak never paused but rushed Anika in a bounding leap. A fur clad nightmare of teeth and claws. Her sword tip pierced one swiping paw ringed in deadly talons, which gave her the briefest breath to swing aside by holding the edge of a rock.

The cat skidded on the snow, spinning itself around and raced at Anika. She stood on solid legs and speared forward with her sword. The cat twisted its head away and ducked under her arm as it moved. Its paw swept at her leg, the claws snagged her leggings, twisting her around and tumbling her over. Tyric watched her roll down the side of the mountain, the snow sticking to her blankets and growing. The cat came directly at him. To save Anika he had to go through the cat.

Tyric charged the cat with his ax high. The cat

curled its body up to use both paws against the blacksmith. Tyric dove under the cat, the snow slick under him. He shot along the ground down the mountain toward Anika. If he overshot her then he would go off the edge of the mountain and she would follow him, encased in snow. He avoided slamming into several boulders by tipping his shoulders and bending his body. Then he came to her. Her boot protruded from the growing snowball and he hooked his elbow around it. His excessive speed attached to her slower movement spun them around and partly up the mountain where he kept hold of her leg. The growing snow packed around her twisted like a top. He brought his ax around and sliced into the snow splitting the ball. The snow disintegrated into chunks that continued down the mountain. Tyric slipped along the mountain dragging Anika by her foot. His arc faded and they slid toward the edge. Tyric dug his boots into the snow and reached for a large gray rock thrusting to the sharp air. He held tight and they stopped.

The Telnak ran toward them, graceful on the snow and wicked in its intent. Tyric shoved his ax into the ice and scooped handfuls of snow, packing them into quick snowballs. He threw them up the mountain so they landed higher than where the cat came to attack them. Anika pushed to her knees and stood up. "That's not going to work."

"Running won't help us. Gives me something to do."

"Humor in the face of danger. I think I can like you more." Anika shuffled her feet in the snow to give a sturdier base and held her sword ready.

The cat neared. Its eyes burned for Tyric. Then the boulders of snow bounded down on it. The first crossed behind the cat. A pair of snowballs rolled across the cat's path and it hopped over them, but when it landed, another rolling snowball struck it. The snow burst against the side of the cat in a shower of snow and knocked the cat to its side. The creature stood and shook its head to clear the snow stuck to its eyelashes and stout whiskers. A third snowball rolled behind those two and punched against the big cat. A fourth snowball hit its rear quarter and spun it around. Then a fifth snowball pinched it between itself and the fourth sticking together and tumbling the frantic cat down the side of the mountain. Its claws failed at gripping the world, leaving slices down the side of the mountain. Tyric thought he saw sparks from the claws when they hit rocks but the cat continued jostling down the mountain toward the last shelf and the edge to nothingness.

Tyric put his hand out to help Anika step closer to himself. They watched as the snow bumped the cat over the edge. He said, "That's good."

Anika nodded.

They heard a shriek that reached through their ears and squeezed black hooks around that little piece of fear along their spines. They looked down at the ledge and saw claws clamp the edge of the rock and the cat pull itself up. It lumbered across the flat ledge and came toward them.

Anika said, "When it gets to us we split to each side. Then attack. It can only choose one. The other must kill it."

Tyric yanked his ax from the ice and crouched. "Good plan. Obvious, but good."

The cat jumped to a lump of yellow stone then the muscles along its whole body flexed, launching it into the air at the two of them. Its lips pulled back from jagged fangs, its lower jaw ready to scoop out both of their bowels in anger. Tyric aimed for its skull but in mid-air the cat leaned back so its front legs stretched out a surprising distance that he realized neither of them could hope to escape. Tyric spun his arm around so it came up under the cat at its neck or chest. He glimpsed Anika's sword chop at the leg on her side of the cat. Tyric's ax struck into the cat's chest through the thick ribs and sliced the cat's heart. Anika's sword struck through the creature's leg at the elbow joint severing most of the tendons and cartilage making that leg useless had Tyric's work not killed the cat. The telnak landed oozing blood into the snow. Then a snap of light and sound crunched across the snow from the cat.

"A wizard? A wizard took the form of a telnak?" Anika shouted. She raised her sword.

The arm of the wizard came from the snow. An orange mist coalesced about him, sucked into his pores and veins. The broken rib-cage knit together and the arm that Anika cut when the wizard still had the cat form, restrung itself with new tendons, muscle, and flesh. He pointed a finger at Anika and she faded to the frozen ground, unconscious. The wizard spoke power into the air. He crawled to his knees, his hand never moving. Something wicked came from that hand, dark and black. The evil cloud stood tall and powerful on the snow near its master. It watched Tyric as it seeped forward. It raised its serrated fists to meet Tyric. The tattoos along Tyric's arms burned in the presence of this powerful magic. He hoped his forge work with Erolok was sufficient. The consuming shadow made him question it as he swung his ax at the constricting black arms that reached for him. He felt the atmosphere boiling with magic. The creature's arm pulled away and his ax only sliced through thin filaments of swirling smoke left in its wake. Then the creature grabbed Tyric's arm with one fist and slammed the other into his body. The punch folded the blacksmith. It flung him up the mountain side. He hit the snow and slid back down toward the monster. It reached for Tyric and took him by the shoulder. It's swirling head stopped and split open on a fragile hinge like a teapot lid but ringed with tunneler teeth. It's throat exposed a glowing red chute filled with hooked teeth all the way down. It inhaled, drawing the free corners of his clothes and the fluttering ends of straps toward those teeth. Its contact with Tyric made him weep. Overwhelming sadness and despair filled him. *Why am I fighting this thing? What good can come of taking this egg to the dragon? This is all so hopeless. I will let it consume me.* The wizard poured his magic and attention into the dark creature, urging it to swallow Tyric. The wizard raised his arms high over his head, a smile broadening his face as Tyric drooped toward the fiery mouth.

A sword blade protruded from the wizard's chest. The wizard looked down, seeing the bright steel tinged with his blood. The wizard's legs folded and he fell to the ground. Anika yanked at her sword and swung it around separating the wizard's head from his body. The head rolled down the mountain gaining snow in its thin hairs where it struck the ledge and bounced into the air. The creature of smoke swirled and dispersed into the winds dropping Tyric to the ground.

"You have tears on your face," Anika said.

Tyric rubbed his cheeks, "Something about that creature. I didn't want to live anymore. I accepted my fate. I welcomed the doom."

"Do you feel like that now?"

Tyric stood up, "No. The fog is clearing." He looked further up the mountain, "We have work to do."

"It's getting dark." Anika slid her foot into Tyric's footprint. Tyric had to kick each foot into the side of the mountain to cut a step and then climb up. Their snowshoes had become useless and they left them behind.

"I feel the temperature dropping again. If it gets any steeper we will need our ropes."

"Too dark for that. Can we find shelter?"

Tyric peered into the gloom. "I see rocks with snow over them – we could dig in."

"Best option I see too." Then Anika clawed at Tyric's shoulder "Back!"

Tyric stopped his forward foot in mid-air. He brought it back to his last footprint, "Another telnak?"

"No. Back further." she tugged at Tyric. When further back, Anika picked up a chunk of ice and heaved it forward, "This is why."

The ice arched upward and struck the snow just ahead of Tyric's last footprint. They did not hear any expected crunch as the ice hit the mountain; instead, a large section of snow disappeared from where the ball went through.

"The snow covers a crack in the mountain. I think we stood on only ice out there and the bubble thinned ahead of us there."

Tyric speared the snow with his ax handle until he felt solid rock below. Then he moved another step and retested the soundness of their path. They saw they had indeed wandered over a snow shelf. "I'm glad you noticed that."

"How many more hidden traps are up the mountain?"

Tyric continued poking the snow and moving up the grade. The end of the crack narrowed until they could step across it.

"That shelter is too far away to go back. I see another ahead that might work. We can dig the snow." Tyric kicked his boot into the snow and climbed. The wind came with a knife edge of chill steel and the snow increased.

Tyric held his ax like a rowboat oar and dug into the snow drift piled between the rocks. The snow slid down the side of the mountain as he worked. The temperature kept dipping deeper with the slicing wind. Tyric's arms flexed and he found pulling the snow out of the quick cave kept him heated, while the mountain slashed its cold knives across his face.

Anika crouched down huddling under her blanket. She kept the edges of the blanket up about her nose so only her eyes watched him. She shivered. "How did it get so cold?"

Tyric reached his hand toward Anika, signaling her to get in the rough cave. She did not dally. Tyric followed her in and scooped more snow from the interior wall blocking up their doorway. The wind swirled with little fingers poking through the slit he left open. The fingers scratched at the edges trying to widen it – hungry for them – wailing over the sharp edges of rocks in frustration.

"That's not normal cold weather."

"I didn't think so either."

The wind moaned around them, deepening in tone and gripping their fears.

"Is it another wizard?"

Tyric closed his eyes, "No. I think this is just the mountain at night this high near the peaks."

Anika said, "The Mountain doesn't really want us here does it?"

"It's just a mountain. It doesn't care. The Enkarian Elven kingdom will be long gone and this mountain will still be here frightening another pair of climbers. For now our snow cave will keep us alive through the night."

"You are sure?"

"You stay up first and I'll get some sleep."

Anika nodded, pulling her knees close to her chest, watching the doorway and the darkness beyond.

Tyric awoke to cold air ripping his face and snow

flecks bouncing on his cheek. He sat up and saw their cave opening pushed aside. He swiveled his head around and Anika was gone!

He unstrapped his ax and burst out of the cave. The wind remained shrill and streaked with snow. He went from being able to see ten feet to seeing across the side of the mountain. Everywhere he looked he saw shifting bands of sleet. Anika's footprints left the cave. Within a few paces, they filled with snow, and a few more they vanished. Tyric looked around and put his hand to his pack. The weight of the pack assured him the dragon egg remained.

Up the slope, he saw the dark shape of a climber, and then the snow obliterated his view. Tyric put away his ax and used both his hands to claw his way after the climber. He hoped it was Anika. Another band of open space between snow bursts showed how far the climber was ahead of him. Tyric hurried.

"What are you doing?" Tyric yelled as he approached Anika. She kept climbing, ignoring his voice. His breath came hard, drawing the cold air like ice needles puncturing the inside of his throat and lungs. "What are you doing?"

Anika remained focused on climbing. Her movements mechanical. Her breathing came as strong as his but she did not wince at the awful pain that ripped his throat and lungs. Tyric came to her and put his hand to her shoulder. Her head swiveled around and her eyes glowed with a steely blue phosphor and seemed to look through him. Her head turned back to her climb, lifting a foot, putting it down, pulling herself up with a hand on a rock, and moving the other foot to a new purchase. She moved up the mountain toward the middle of the twin peaks. Tyric climbed faster ahead and remained between her and the center of those peaks. Anika did not falter from a direct line to that place unless a large rock blocked her way. Tyric did not know what drove her but it seemed best to leave her on her path. He would get to her destination first – but what would he find? What wizard is up here?

A diagonal slice appeared in the space where the two mountain peaks joined. Tyric thought it looked like the crack at the root of mill gears after they fractured under excessive load. The opening proved much wider as he came closer than he could see where Anika climbed. He stepped inside the cave and the air smelled moist and his lungs stopped hurting. Tyric almost tasted something in the air upon is tongue, pleasant like cedars under fresh snow but a thread of bitter danger threaded through it.

Tyric stood inside the lip of the cave, his ax free, and watched Anika finish climbing the mountain. He listened to the murmur of the winds mixed with the tinkling flake-ice that swirled around the edges of the tunnel. The tunnel twisted into the darkness of the mountain depths. He touched her shoulder when she entered the cave but she only continued deeper into the darkness. He tugged on her icy hand. Her fingers wiggled free of his after giving him another stare with those steel eyes and she walked further into the mountain. Tyric gripped her face with his hands, "Anika, it's me, wake up." Her eyes flashed at him but she kept moving forward. Tyric remembered the King's statements about the fairy tales and he kissed her chilled lips, melting the crust of frost filling the edges of her mouth. Her hand pushed him away. She walked forward, unblinking and silent into the blackness wrapping the cavern ahead. Tyric's mind dropped to his gem to illuminate the way with a low light. They walked along and Tyric saw how very little rubble covered the floor. The walls and ceiling and the floor showed evidence of long scything marks, similar to the dwarves' mining tools but much greater arcs cut in. The tunnel did follow the regular rectangular shape of the dwarves but left coarse and unfinished with an irregular shape that curled like artwork hammered into a sword. The tunnel gave the feeling of balance as if its creator had purposefully dug it rough but to a detailed plan. The mountain rumbled and breathed its breath of cedars but dryer like the air several steps away from a forge fire. The tunnel bent while the ceiling reached up more than he could accurately measure. Anika continued following its meandering path deeper into the mountain. Tyric felt a tug upon him, not in his body but through his mind. Danger alarms fired all along his spine and wiggled up his scalp but he too stepped forward. A look along the bright edge of his dagger eased his thoughts that his eyes did not glow like hers. He felt free will to stop, but somewhat troubled by why he did not stop and tie Anika down or do something other than following her into whatever lived beyond – in the blackness of this mountain. Even if he suspected this might be the dragon's cave they searched for.

A glowing light burned ahead in the darkness as they trudged around the last bend. The way opened into a great cavern filled with sucking black beyond the fringe of the far lamp and Tyric's light. The blackness so complete between them there could be a wide chasm and Tyric would not see it until too late. What shadows crept around them? What creatures clung to the walls and ceiling that he could not see? Anika walked toward the light. The mountain rumbled around them, low and inaudible except for the feeling through his boots.

A great eye cracked open and pierced the darkness brighter than the lamp near it. The eye looked from Anika to fix on Tyric. He saw the bright vertical iris flex as the eye focused on him, large and round behind a lid under an angular brow that could be quick to anger. Depths of blues with flecks of yellows surrounded a soul extracting blackness inside the pupil. The eye moved across him studying his physical presence with such strength it might even be looking through him. A voice spoke, seeming to bang about in his chest while it shouted through his mind, "Who are you to climb upon my mountain?"

Anika stopped and stood statue still.

The dragon said to Tyric, "I asked who you are? And why does my spell not make you docile like this woman?"

Tyric stowed his ax, not remembering when he might have taken it in his hand. The dragon seemed impervious to it and carrying it might only split a dangerous discussion. "I don't know why I keep from your spell."

The dragon raised its head, both eyes now focused on him, "I think you do know."

"Perhaps. I'll share it if you free her."

"She is quite safe. I have only one fool I need to talk with. How came you to my mountain?"

"The King of the Enkarian Elves sent me to find you."

"King Ek has been mad for many years. He sent you on a fool's quest," talons scrapped in the darkness, nearing them but still unseen and Tyric guessed the source of the cavern's mysterious carving design. What kind of armor would he need to survive a strike by weapons that cut through stone? The dragon said, "But the King is now dead. His wizard son sits on the throne."

Tyric stepped back startled that the King was dead. "We did not know the king had perished. How do you know?"

"A dragon has methods, and centuries to perfect them." The talons dug into the rock emphasizing the last row of defenses that keep a dragon alive that long. "I smelled you across the swamps and then up the mountain. You survived the hazards."

"Were they yours?" Tyric asked.

"Mine? No. That is Shadow Wizard magic. Old magic. Well, I say that because it's old for you. You have a faster sense of time than I do. That magic is from another world when the land was dangerous, even for dragons. I fear someone has found his magic again. There are so few dragons now." Tyric felt the dragon's sorrow. "Dragons lived in so many parts of the world then, magnificent dragons, heroic dragons. Too many perished in the War."

Sadness washed over Tyric and seemed to soak his

skin like a misty rain. Tears blurred his eyes. He saw dragons slashing on the battle fields, burning among fires and the purple lightning reaching above the korlak hordes to wrench the dragons from the sky. Monsters conjured by wizards that only a dragon's nightmare might conceive. He saw the dragons dying. He felt the splash of an icy tear upon the stone. "You fought in that war?"

"We lost too many. The costs were high. Fortunate for us all that Aleron and the Kelvin Mage ended that war."

"King Ek sent me to find you and return something you lost."

"I have not lost anything the King of the Elves could have found. I have not lost anything in centuries. Many kings would have come and gone."

"You need to release Anika before I will share it."

"It is safer for me to only talk with one of you. You brought it? I could just take it." The dragon's talon scraped into Tyric's light. The steely black talon looked like a new sword freshly quenched in burning oil and polished for field battle.

Tyric's fingers twitched for his ax but he stilled them. "I could negotiate holding the item I brought you in as much danger as you give her. We will stay at an impasse until one of us gives in. But if you are not an ally then this is indeed a fool's errand." Tyric slung his pack from his back to the floor. He reached for the flap.

The dragon's talon clicked up off the stone, "Careful, human."

"How good is the word of a dragon?"

"Only as good as the moment. When you live for centuries, you have more at stake than the lives of brief but numerous flies. Consistent adherence to a ludicrous sense of upholding an honor code or a rigid opinion can mean death."

Tyric tipped the pack over exposing the egg.

The dragon's eyes narrowed, disbelieving the lightly glowing sphere that lay among the spilled blankets. The dragon said softly, "The egg!" Tyric felt the darkness shift as the dragon moved. Small platinum reflections revealed the curves of the creature that measured triple the size of the one he fought from the wizard's cloak. The dragon's smooth skin stayed tight and never showed a wrinkle. A purr throbbed through the air as her talons caressed the small orb, turning it over. "The glow still lives!" Waves of sadness, joy, exuberance, and sorrow spilled through Tyric from the dragon. His legs trembled and he staggered, catching himself on his knee. The dragon rolled its smooth head slightly in the light that increased like the glow of dawn, "I thought she was lost."

Tyric lifted his head, "How was the egg lost?" Waves of sadness struck him as tattered images of heavy wounds ripped through the dragon guarding a clutch of eggs. She watched them take her eggs away. A dragon helpless to save them. The Shadow Wizard's twisted face poured power into spells and creatures that struck the dragon. Tyric put his hands to his head but he could not push the disorientated images and emotions away. His lids clamped tight over his eyes and he retreated to his mind. The blue fire of his gem burned sharp and crisp among the images consuming his thoughts. The blue burned brighter into a pale swirling mist that wrapped his form. The other images faded and he pushed the mist outward. Amid the burning smoke and wizardry, a green sward of life expanded around him and shoved the feelings away. Calm waves lapped on the lake shore and bird songs drowned the wailing beasts. Tyric raised himself to standing, his hands dropped away and he opened his eyes to look at the dragon. He had thrown the darkness back from the room.

The dragon whispered, while its talons gently caressed the egg, "Aleron's son!" She sniffed, "He promised he would help me. But he died by the Shadow Wizard before he ever could."

Anika stirred and inhaled a sharp breath, "Where are we?"

Tyric said, "You have been under this dragon's spell."

Anika's feet went to a battle stance, her sword drawn and ready.

Tyric said, "You won't need that."

The dragon bowed her head. "The Children of Aleron have returned."

Tyric said, "I have no family."

"By choice?" the dragon asked.

Tyric said, "I only remember being apprenticed. Never any family."

"You have one of the gems." The dragon coiled its head closer, "Let me see it."

Tyric pulled his gauntlet off and showed the ring on his fist to the dragon. Her eyes scanned it. "Yes.

That is one of the gems. The others are scattered. He did it then."

"Did what?"

"Deep magic. Strong magic. He feared for his family, even after the Shadow Wizard appeared defeated. Maybe Aleron wasn't killed by the Shadow Wizard but died putting you here."

"A thousand years in the future?"

"Aleron could see the future. He must have known the Shadow Wizard would survive and return. Strong magic."

Anika asked, "How do you know so much about King Aleron?"

The dragon said, "I fought in that war with Aleron. A King of Kings. He wore an armband studded with magical stones. I see that gem in your ring is one of them." Her head swung closer to Tyric, "You can control light and push away the darkness. Can you make a shield wall and heal the wounded?"

"I made an iron shield on the mountain. I have not healed anyone," Tyric looked at the stone in his ring, "I should study it more."

"That ring is why my spells did not work on you, and why other magic has not been effective against you." The dragon looked at her closed talons, "Like this egg – that gem – is a potent weapon for the Shadow Wizard or whoever found his magic. Aleron did well hiding them. That must be why the elves kept the egg instead of giving it to me sooner –"

"It was hidden at Emperor's Keep. The elves may have only known where it was kept."

"Too much risk giving it to me earlier." The dragon stroked the sides of the egg, "She will have a longer life since it has not started yet. I will have to think on this. The world has turned dangerous again. I've seen the kelvin at war with the korlak, wizards battle in the extinct Snowy Elf lands. Magic released from hidden holes deep under the Monastery of Zan. Siblings of yours with Aleron's gems are fighting. Surviving and dying."

Anika asked, "So you will help us?"

"You must stay here with the egg. I will need wood for a fire nest." The dragon slid toward the cavern entrance.

"Wait! You will leave us here?"

"I will return soon. I know where one of the forge fire trees has grown against the hills. I will not be long." The dragon slipped from the cavern and launched like glimmering fluid mercury from the face of the mountain.

Tyric and Anika stood in the silence of the cave with the glowing egg stirring at their feet.

The dragon returned with two thick branches gripped in its rear talons that it dragged into the cavern scraping like witches brooms. The dragon cracked the dense wood in its talons to fashion a small pile. When satisfied with the shape of the wood pile she swung her snout into the crossed wood. With a rush and a snap, tiny flames ignited from the sides of the dragon's mouth. The blistering flames burned near invisible white-blue jets that, even though tiny, burst heat across them like Tyric's forge stoked to soften steel slabs in the middle of the hot damp summer. Tyric and Anika stepped away from the heat. The dragon blew on the egg with puffs that increased the intensity of the flame forcing Tyric and Anika further back.

The egg glowed red. The dragon increased the temperature until the brightest white blazed beyond a lightning arc white and still the heat increased. The air around the egg sparkled as it too began to burn. Tyric had never seen any flame so hot. He closed his eyes and the image flared. He looked away and opened his eyes to the cavern walls and the massive room previously hidden in darkness flickered and glowed brighter than the sun-scattered snow. Anika walked and then ran toward the wall. Tyric's armor boiled and he fled with her. They scratched at the stone hoping it remained cool but the rock was already hot and dry.

Tyric groped for Anika's hand and pulled her behind him. He remembered where the exit might be. His chest tightened under the heat. He feared they might not escape. The tunnel barely protected them from the super heated air expanding and pushing outward, drawing air out of their lungs and their breaths in too painful to do more than sip at the air. Anika stumbled. Tyric kept hold of Anika's hand and pulled her after him. The long tunnel had shortened on his blurry pace out of the heat. He swung Anika passed the lip of the cave opening and spun himself over the edge. The snow felt cool against his body and steam rose from him. He wanted to strip out of his armor but he just allowed the snow to quench the metal. He rubbed snow against Anika's face and hands since she still seemed groggy. He scooped up dripping snow and splashed it against her face.

Anika coughed.

"You're awake." Tyric's boot slipped in the slushy snow. He regained his balance.

Anika pushed at the snow, "Why is the mountain melting?"

Tyric looked at the cave mouth. The heated air oozed out in shimmering bands as cold air sucked along the bottom of the opening to replace it. The snow around the cave mouth melted. The heat seeping further and further along the face of the mountain. The ground under the two of them softened and shifted. Dust and debris locked in the snow and ice melted into a slurry that began sliding in drips, then small rivulets, and then in clumps and sheets.

Tyric pulled at Anika and he threw her down inside the cavern where the cool air sucked into the opening. They crawled back inside of the dripping ice and any dangerous snow hanging over the opening to the cavern. "A little further. We do not want to be caught in the mountain slipping off its face."

An avalanche thundered next to the cave mouth. Then another let lose and streamed across the cave opening as if they hid in a grotto under a waterfall. The mountain side shot over the giant steps in bubbling bursts of spray. "If we stood a safe distance away in the woods, this snow and water would look spectacular." Anika said, lying on her back breathing the cool moist air that rushed passed them. "How long do you think this will go on?"

Tyric asked, "Did you ever have chickens sitting on eggs?"

"No."

"Then no idea."

Anika reached for Tyric's hand and gripped it, "Thank you."

"For what?"

"We're involved in something important." Anika laughed. "– if we survive, of course."

They felt the cave shake and the dragon moved out of the tunnel. The great dragon stopped and lowered its head, "Meet Crystal." They could feel the heat still radiating off the dragon.

A tiny dragon, delicate in every way compared to its full grown mother, with little talons like mouse's feet, jumped from the dragon's snout to the ground. It rushed forward until it neared Tyric and Anika. Then it stretched its neck out and sniffed at them, looking them over with its alien eyes. Tyric put his hand out to the dragon as if letting a rugged mastiff smell him to determine friend or foe. The little dragon nodded and moved closer to Anika to smell her and then it came back to Tyric. It nuzzled its nose against Tyric's hand. Tyric cautiously ran his fingers over the side of the dragon's head and neck."Smooth and soft you are, Crystal."

The dragon said, "She will not be for long. Crystal, you will travel with Tyric."

Anika asked, "A baby dragon traveling with us?"

The dragon seemed to shrug, "You carried her as an egg. She is much less fragile now."

Anika said, "Look at those tiny talons and that long pretty tail."

The dragon said, "She'll shed soon with the next growth spurt."

Crystal purred. Tyric knelt before the baby dragon and she licked his face. Anika laughed. Tyric stroked his hands along Crystal's head, which warmed to his touch. He asked, "Why are you sending your baby with us? Even if she is more durable now?"

"The Shadow Wizard's magic is upon the land again." The dragon's eyes looked out the cavern across the world. Tyric knew she could see to the real horizon with such clarity she likely watched the lizards and bugs flit about at that far edge of the world. "You are Aleron's son and I know pieces of the destiny he foresaw. He wept so after the first of the visions. I only know you will help fight the evil. You must have the Enkarian Elves for this new war. They are slipping under the spells of that Prince Frael who would call himself King only because he murdered his father." Tyric sensed anger swelling in the dragon. Then a calmness as wizardry of her own melded into a slip of stone curved like a small boat or a plate that lifted from the floor, "Climb in. You too, Crystal."

Tyric hesitated at the edge of the stone. The baby dragon bounced inside like a dog in a departing wagon. "This is a sled down the mountain?"

The dragon rumbled, "This will fly you down the mountain and a short way into the forest. That is as far as my magic can take it."

"If you came with us it would help," Anika suggested.

"No. I have work to begin here. You do not want to be near when that happens. I expect I will destroy much of the mountain practicing my old magic. Or not. It depends on what I can remember. I have also been slumbering much too long and the old body needs better fitness."

Tyric asked, "What to feed Crystal? How to care for her?"

"Feed her magic, the rest she will know what to do. Growing dragons need magic."

"But I have no magic, I am not a wizard."

"Korlak wizards seek you. Their magic will make her grow strong. Even in the egg, she gathered some of the magic the wizards flung around you during your journey here. The korlak search for you across the forest. I saw them scale the mountains and stalk the giant steps for you when I returned with the firewood."

Anika said, "Magic from wizards that try to destroy us?" She climbed into the little craft and the dragon closed her eyes and lifted them off. Harsh winds again blew across the face of the mountain.

Tyric scanned the liquid water that had flashed again into a smooth sheet of ice all down the mountain face, "We could never have climbed down over that."

Anika looked at the wall, "We could have, but slow. This is better."

The wind buffeted the boat as much as waves in a storm but they remained cupped inside as the craft lowered into the forest. Crystal bounded out when the hull touched the soil and she ran along the underbrush. "Crystal! Wait!"

The baby dragon raced back, rounded them and climbed up a thick tree trunk. It leaped from that three to another yards away, scampered higher, then jumped to the ground, circling Anika and Tyric three more times. She stopped and sat on her haunches, crunching the last of a bird and swallowing. Her head tilted toward Tyric, waiting.

Tyric said, "I guess we need to find out what happened at the castle. Even if they hunt us."

"Perhaps we will surprise them coming to the castle instead of fleeing?" Anika walked ahead.

"Remember, the dragon suggested a direct assault upon the castle and the wizards to ensure growing the baby dragon with their magic. Not for our convenience."

"Oh."

The peaks of the mountains behind them boomed with noise from the dragon.

Chapter XVIII: Brothers

"Brother, what have you done?" Prince Elraf set his helmet on the table, the clink of the metal on the marble echoed through the empty chamber. Empty of anyone but the two brothers and the old artifacts of their father's kingdom, freshly polished and still smelling of lemon.

The wizard tapped the crown on his head, "Seems father favored me to rule as King."

"Convenient that father died while I chased that escaped murderer Tyric through the forest."

King Frael said, "One can never tell in these things. When the mind twists its last grip on the world."

"What did your hand have in the affair?" Prince Elraf asked.

"You're accusing me of participating in murder?"

"It's a possibility. Rumors exist that you forced him to sign. You have motive to precipitate such an event."

"My brother," King Frael smiled, "You are too paranoid. Or you are searching for reasons why our esteemed father might have given the crown to me and not to you."

"I understand your wizard powers may influence the balance of power, but he kept the throne as long as he did because he lacked trust in either of us. That was no secret – among all of our other secrets."

The wizard nodded, "Those secrets are deep, I

agree." His fingers traced the depths of the carvings in the chair he sat in, "Please, have a seat. I offer it again."

"No. Since you have the administration of the kingdom now, I do not need to be involved. I will attempt finding the trail of our murderer anew and ensure that issue is closed. I am weary of this. I will leave for the beaches of Kytran Bay. Wine by the sultry ocean will be a good change for me." He touched the bandage covering his nose, wondering if perhaps Tyric had improved its shape.

"Wishing for faraway lands is nice, but the world is changing."

"If the weight of that crown gets too heavy, you will know where to find me."

"Those sandy beaches will not be so idyllic. Even they will churn red with danger. Very soon." The wizard lifted a staff Prince Elraf had not seen laying across his brother's lap. "I have this new weapon and I find it very powerful."

"That is not –"

"Yes. It's a Shadow Staff, lost in –"

"– Lost in the Great War. I heard the same stories from our father. How did you manage to locate it?"

"You remember I researched these ancient weapons that destroyed so many armies of the elves. It came by way of the mountains."

"Who would trade anything for one of those?"

"A few have needs that align with our purposes."

"That is powerful magic. Dangerous magic. I can sense it from here and I never completed the basic wizardry training."

"You had enough to understand the beginnings."

"Enough to know the dangers and the risks. I wondered why the room seemed charged, I thought a parlor trick of yours attempting to impress me."

"I have no need to impress anyone." The end of the staff glowed with a purple phosphorescence. "You remember the purple lightning of the stories?"

"Yes."

"That lightning is not a mere story." The end of the staff crackled with electricity. The air about it hissed and popped.

Prince Elraf stepped away from the table, his hand clutching his helmet, wondering if his brother prepared to kill him, "What did you bargain for?"

"A bargain it certainly is, but just a token of more to come. I'm ensuring the safety of the elves when the next war comes."

"The next war?"

"Have you not paid attention to how the land is changing? Have you not seen creatures absent since the time the Shadow Wizard nearly ruled the world?"

Prince Elraf said, "Tunnelers and mountain dogs do not make for an apocalypse."

"I know what is ahead. We do not have the weapons and armor that our fathers had when they fought beside Aleron. They had those weapons and armor and nearly became as extinct as our cousins the Snowy Elves. We have had peace for too long and our people are too soft. The danger forgotten. Few know how to make the weapons of old. Fewer still to wage the wars."

"We have a full armory."

"And more weapons than brave arms to hold them. Weapons, if you can call them that. Forgotten implements less sharp than the farmer's tools used to grub in the earth. Weapons disintegrating in moldering ruin. They will not survive the shock of first battle."

"Those weapons are tougher than you think."

"I have carried this fear since I saw the first signs." King Frael said, "We will survive, the elves of this wood have always survived. We owe our people that they survive – as their leaders. I am ensuring our success."

"You are too dramatic."

"Am I? What did you plan to do when our kingdom is attacked? I have seen a dragon over the forest. Old dangers lurk in every crevice of the mountains and shadowed timber stand."

"That is what we train for. I train our army myself at our monthly practice sessions. While you hide in your tower and –"

"– in my tower learning magic that will save our kingdom when we are attacked. You remember learning maps as children. We are on the east border of this whole land. The range of mountains beside our forests gives us the only protective wall against the korlak lands. When they have a strong leader and build cohesive armies, they cannot attack us because of that mountain range. The old powers," he twisted the staff in his fingers, "Could take them over and under the mountains. Those old powers are returning to the land. The advanced korlak scouts have come, and worse creatures too."

"You just fear ghosts too long dead, brother."

"I was unable to convince our father. Fortunately he bequeathed the kingdom to me so I have the power to properly prepare."

Prince Elraf waved his helmet, "Don't spend all the castle's gold building up stores against an enemy that will never appear." He walked away but paused at the door, "I think I will leave finding the murderous Tyric to you. I am starting my vacation early. Good luck, brother."

"Enjoy yourself. That blacksmith problem is nearly resolved anyway."

"Curious events with that one. Why that Rubied Assassin stays with him, I cannot guess – but I suspect you can – since you advise their guild?"

"You know I am only involved in that guild to ensure we are not surprised by plotting usurpers."

Prince Elraf held his hand on the edge of the door, "At least not any plotters we don't know."

The purple glow around the staff crackled and spit, the only sound in the chamber besides the slam of the plank door. The wizard sighed and peered out the window. The ridge of mountains thrust above the trees like a dragon's jaw jagged with impending doom, "Where are you hiding, Tyric the blacksmith?"

Chapter XIX: The Way Home

Crystal rubbed her head against Tyric's thigh, the smooth features of her armor sliding along his armor. "Shh. Stay still, Crystal." He could not believe how fast she grew. The size of a goat now. Tyric waited in the fading sunlight as it dipped over the edge of the forest. The smell of smoke filtered through the brush from the korlak camp along with unsavory odors from bubbling pots over low fires of green wood. Sooty smoke rose to the tree tops. A vile dinner cooked by vile creatures. The camp had been hacked clear from the brush. Tyric nodded to Anika who moved around the tree from behind them. She took another position further ahead.

"Come," Tyric whispered to the little dragon, his hand pulling at her neck. Crystal followed him, sniffing the air. She stopped before a tree that Tyric passed. The dragon sniffed at a black mark etched into the bark with wizard flame. Tyric turned, "Come." He stepped back to touch the dragon and she snapped at the edge of chain mail hanging at his waist and pulled him back.

Anika came back to them, "What is going on? We talked about going around them but we didn't want them attacking us from behind, especially if we got pinched between them and something else ahead."

Crystal snorted and pointed her nose at the mark on the tree.

Anika looked at the mark, "Wizard script."

"It's on that tree over there, and the one ahead." Tyric said to Anika, "Warnings?"

"I see them now on most of the trees."

Tyric released his ax, "Which of these are markers and which are traps?"

"All of them are different shapes." Anika put a finger out to touch the charred figure, "I wonder what it smells like? Maybe that will give us a clue?" Her finger touched the mark and an explosion of electricity burst from the tree. Other trees around the perimeter of the camp burst in a cascading chain that circled their enemy. The electricity pounded into Tyric and Anika knocking them to the ground. Korlak in battle gear streamed from the woven huts in camp. Tyric and Anika got to their feet shaking their heads to clear the magic induced stupor. They lost the ability to surprise the korlak but the closeness of the trees here funneled the korlak to them. Anika's sword sliced through the first korlak. Tyric saw their armor was regular light field issue. They easily deflected the korlak swords in the narrow space. Another tent of korlak approached rapidly while a wizard readied some sort of spell.

Anika grabbed a dagger from the korlak she cut down. She spun, kicked another korlak, and threw the dagger across the camp at the korlak wizard. The dagger sunk in the wizard's stomach. She fished another dagger from the next korlak she killed and threw that one at the wizard. The point stabbed through a lung a hand's breadth higher than the first dagger. The wizard wrenched the first dagger out and tried pulling the second, finding it wedged into his fractured rib. The korlak gripped its hands around the dagger handle forgetting its spells.

Tyric hacked into another korlak with his ax so deep his face met the korlak's growling visage. He cranked the ax handle and kicked the korlak from his weapon as it tried feebly clapping its swords against him. Anika's next dagger throw split through the wizard's wrist pinning it to his chest. Tyric sheared through the breastplate of a korlak nearing Anika's side. Tyric's ax flailed, sliced, and probed the korlak troop. Several tried protecting the wizard with their shields. Tyric stabbed the points of his ax into a shield and twisted it away, exposing the wizard. His next swing hacked the muscles from the wizard's shoulder. The shields closed the gap again in front of the wizard, but too late, "No spells from you today," he said.

Anika came beside him and they moved around the camp. With the wizard threat largely removed, they dispatched the remaining korlak quickly. Only the two shield bearers and the wizard remained. Anika stayed slightly behind and to the side of Tyric as they approached the shielded wizard. The shields parted as Tyric came close. Purple lightning shot through the gap and struck his ax. The ax flew out of his hands tumbling through the air to sink into a rotten log at the side of the camp. The wizard stood, whole and healed. Another bolt of electricity reached for Tyric. Tyric felt the dragon rush behind him and connect her head with his armor. The lightning struck Tyric but the energy raced across his metal armor and sunk into the dragon. The hairs on Tyric's body stood on end but he only felt the rough vibration of the current conducting around him. The wizard's eyes widened but he whipped his arms back and forward again with a lash of energy from his hands, one at Tyric and the other at Anika. The dragon pressed its head firmly against Tyric, making Tyric stumble to maintain his footing while her long tail flipped around Anika's body where the bolt of energy would hit her. All faster than Tyric or Anika could think.

The energy entered the dragon from both of them. Then it turned, hooting into the air. A grin upon its mouth filled with sharp teeth as it dropped its gaze back to the wizard. The dragon walked toward the wizard. Tyric and Anika rushed forward after Tyric retrieved his ax. The korlak clamped their shields together.

The wizard shot electricity directly at the dragon that continued forward until her nose came against the wizard. She butted her head into the wizard and sprang on his sprawling body. Ripping teeth tore through the korlak's body and ripped its heart from shattered ribs. In a single gulp, the dragon swallowed the still beating heart. The dragon turned to Tyric and smiled its mouth full of sharp teeth, colored in dripping blood. The dragon raced around several trees. Then came back to Tyric and nuzzled his thigh.

"Glad she likes us." Anika put her sword away.

* * *

"Another korlak camp." Anika gripped the handle of her sword "Are they overrunning the forests now?"

Crystal sniffed at a wizard mark scrawled up a tree

near them. Tyric pulled at the dragon's neck. Two korlak came from the tent in the center of a cluster of coarse woven brush huts. The korlak used green bushes that since dried brown and hung with dead leaves to build their huts. A wizard held a glowing ball over clenched fists while the second korlak held the wizard's staff. "We must have tripped something already, they know we are here."

Other armored korlak burst from the huts dressed in full armor. The wizard pulled his fists apart, a crack of thunder ripped from the sky.

Anika threw one of the daggers she had collected from the korlak bodies at the first camp at the korlak wizard as it released the pulsating sphere toward them. Thunder crackled across the sky as the dagger struck the korlak wizard's stomach. The blade broke the wizard's concentration and the sphere pulsated into nothingness.

Tyric collided with the first korlak, gouging long gashes into the sides of its horny red armor but doing no damage to the creature. The korlak wizard thumped the butt of his staff on the ground. A vitriol of red, green, and black spurted from the forest leaf bed to ooze with scorching flames toward Tyric as a wavering cloud of gas spindled from it.

Anika threw another dagger and the korlak next to the wizard brought his shield up and protected the wizard.

The korlak spun a long red-bladed sword against Tyric. Tyric bounced the korlak's first blow with his ax and brought his weapon around, slicing across the armor of the korlak's torso. A second cut in the same spot would penetrate. Tyric chipped at the shoulder armor as the korlak's sword pommel-nut crunched into his helmet. Tyric stumbled back until he shook the ringing from his head; he regained his footing and attacked the korlak's torso again.

Anika dodged under the next swing to lunge for the korlak's chest, but the red sword struck and sliced through Anika's sword. Surprised, she looked at the clean cut edge revealing the korlak's sword flowed with magic. The korlak ripped a dagger from its belt and brought it under Anika's arm, chewing into her ribs. Anika fell back wheezing and spitting blood and collapsed to the ground.

Tyric watched Anika fall but the korlak's red sword came around to him. He smashed his ax against the flat of the sword, forcing it down. Then he kicked at the korlak knocking it back.

Vines as thick as saplings entwined Crystal's legs and partway up her body. There the vines ended in ragged ruin where the dragon chewed at them. The korlak wizard displayed the staff and the ground rumbled below the roots of the trees.

The korlak brought the red sword around in a blur and hit against the edge of Tyric's ax. If he doubted the metal of his weapon, he knew now it stood strong. He had forged it but his Elven blacksmith teacher helped him put the deeper magic into it. Many of the runes marked on his arms came from that forging. He still felt the memory of the burns putting them in his skin. He knew he had more training and more artwork necessary on his body but he was close to finishing that training.

He beat against the sword again and kicked the korlak's knee. Then his shoulder brought around the heavy ax and he bit through the korlak's shoulder armor, dropping the sword with its useless arm attached.

A second korlak came from the shadows of a black tree trunk and swung another magic sword at Tyric. The sword smashed into his upper arm, slicing into armor and flesh. The korlak slammed its body forward with a blow that knocked Tyric down. Tyric could see Anika laying in the leaves. He reached out for her and the ax that had fallen from his hand.

The korlak laughed, it shook its sword free from its severed arm and bore down on Tyric. Tyric rolled to the side as the red blade plunged to the hilt in the dark soil. Tyric scratched at the forest floor toward his ax.

The sod welled and split in front of Crystal. A hand of molten rock gripped the edge of the hole to pull itself free. The dragon growled a sound that pricked at their bodies but not as deeply as her mother's did in the cave. The magma creature flamed the drier leaves next to its feet as it reached for the dragon. The dragon arched her neck back until the creature came within her range. Then she struck at it, biting into the flaming rock and crunching through its shoulder and neck. Tyric saw the creature shudder and the flames wink out – as if the dragon had extinguished a candle. He saw her fling the dead husk of the creature aside and pull one leg from the vines. "You are getting stronger, Crystal."

Two korlak slashed at Tyric who rolled away from each. They drove him further from his ax at each move.

The korlak maneuvered themselves between him and his ax as they harassed him with their swords. Tyric moved back until his boots struck against a black tree. Further retreat seemed impossible. Tyric worried Anika lay dead but he could not reach her. He glanced at her and saw three korlak approaching her with drawn knives, pointing with gap-toothed grins on their faces.

Crystal stepped from the still twining vines and came toward the wizard. Tyric closed his eyes and remembered the iron shield he made on the side of the mountain. He pushed those thoughts through his gem and the shell crunched down on the forest floor shielding Anika. The edge of the shield crushed the korlak approaching her.

The second korlak swung its sword at Tyric's prior wound. Tyric wound his arm around the striking sword, clamping it against his body even as it cut into it. He rotated his body bending the sword around and pulling it from the grip of the korlak. He plucked the sword from his side and backhanded it through the korlak. The red blade of the first korlak missed Tyric and gashed into the tree, the tree cracked with a noise felt through their boots more than with their ears and it toppled over.

Tyric brought the sword around and speared the korlak. One of the three korlak that merged upon Tyric retrieved the magic sword from the dead body. Tyric ran for his ax. He kicked its head, flipping the handle up to his hand and threw the ax at the korlak with the red sword.

A vein of darkness spread around the dragon from the wizard's staff. The dragon writhed in the pain from the black cloud. Power more than she could cope with. Korlak fighters approached her as she fell to her knees and rolled like a slaughtered calf upon the ground, their swords raised to finish the dragon.

Tyric's ax split the korlak's head and chest. The body fell back. The korlak rushing behind it and plucked the falling sword from their comrade and raced at Tyric. One of the other korlak snatched at Tyric's ax but found it too cumbersome to use, so it dropped it to the ground.

The korlak sliced back and forth with the red sword. Tyric put his hand up, channeling his mind through his ring and a second shield expanded before him and crunched down into the forest floor. Freed from his attackers, Tyric ran for his ax. He heard them banging from the inside but knew they could not get out. They might dig their way but that would be slow. Tyric saw the regular swords of the korlak seemed useless against the dragon, but several daggers of theirs bore the same red metal and wizard forge marks as the sword used against him. Those weapons pierced the dragon's armored skin. Crystal flopped back and forth with the pile of korlak upon her like hunting lions. They could kill her before long.

Tyric swung his ax and chopped through two of the dragon's attackers. The wizard oozed more of the black fog that sought Tyric but the fog faded when it reached him. Tyric struck at another korlak and then another, focusing on those with the magic weapons. Tyric wanted to grab a second weapon but his arm remained mostly useless, painfully throbbing, and his side dripped red. He focused his mind through his arm and the ax and jumped over Crystal's whipping tail. He slashed another korlak and then another with his ax. He kicked a third away with his boot and took another's head off. Then he speared the fallen korlak as it tried to get to its feet. Only the wizard remained in the camp. The wizard spun another spell from its staff, a purple cloud of lightning dripping orange fog with each blast against the ground stalking toward Tyric. Tyric walked forward, the magic dissipating around him until he stood before the wizard. The korlak's eyes narrowed in spite and he thrust a red dagger at Tyric. Tyric stabbed the arm with his ax then swung it hard in a loop that cut through the staff and the wizard. An explosion of wizardry escaped from the broken staff. Tyric turned away from the blast and raced to Anika, the shield around her fading as he approached.

Tyric knelt beside her. His ear close to her mouth. A faint breath touched his face. "You live!" But he did not know how long. Her wounds ran her life into the dried leaves with a red brighter than any leaf in the fall. His wounded hand rested lightly upon her forehead, feeling the changing autumn in her. "Anika, what can I do?" The korlak clanged against the steel that trapped them. Tyric rested his forehead on her shoulder, tears welled along his lower lid. Always strong and resourceful, his mind gave him a blank solution. Her body moved with the floppy softness of a freshly killed rabbit. He did not know what to do. Then the dragon's question in the cave came to him, *Can you ... heal the wounded?* Pain for Anika rent through his chest. He drew a deep breath and pulled his head from her shoulder. He pressed his hand against her heart and closed his eyes, pushing his mind through his gem. He saw the blackness of her wounds, from the massive one in her rib cage down to the little scrapes and slices given by the cloying underbrush during their journey through the wood. His mind touched at the ragged edges of her tears and smoothed across them. The flesh wove itself together by wiggling and pulling the muscles together. Strands of bone reached for the other side of their breaks and pulled themselves together like boatmen pulled ropes when docking a heavy ship. Her whole body glowed under his hands. He watched his own body knit itself anew in pace with hers.

Anika's hand reached up and touched Tyric's face, "We must be dead?"

"No, very much alive."

"But you glow and I do not feel my wounds. I grow stronger." She looked around the forest, "Our enemies are dead and we appear unharmed."

"The dragon told me of a power I never knew I possessed." Tyric rubbed the back of his fingers against her cheek. "I must see if I can mend Crystal." He rose to his feet and went to the dragon who breathed in halted gasps from the many wounds littering her silvered body. His mind worked at her wounds. Quickly, the dragon rose and shook her head clear. She snorted and nuzzled the side of Tyric's head. "You are welcome, Crystal."

Anika asked, "Who is under the shield?"

"I think you can guess."

Anika said, "We are not done yet."

"No." Tyric hefted his ax. He strode toward the

noisy shield and faded it but brought it back, isolating one korlak at a time. The last one he brought free of the shield swung the red sword. Tyric blocked the strike with his ax then hacked across the korlak's body separating the creature in two.

Tyric lifted the red sword from the leaves and gave it to Anika, "You need a new sword. A few daggers around here match this. You should keep those too."

"Why did they drag that log this far?"

Tyric whispered, "Special trees for special purposes."

"Easy to track them here."

Tyric nodded. They crouched below a rotting log that remained covered in ferns that spilled down the small ridge the log tumbled down long ago. Crystal lounged along the log, her eyes closed as if she rested but Tyric knew she listened to the noise of the logging camp. Wizards tended a tall saw gang lifted by demon-like monsters with tentacles. Others dragged logs from the forest in a long procession into work stations. They peeled off the bark then split the log or cut it into sections. Then other stations banded cut boards together that the korlak dragged south through the forest.

"They are lumbering out the forest."

"Why does our King not stop them? Obviously their bonfires burning the bark and scab limbs could be seen all the way to the castle."

Tyric suggested, "Did they somehow get permission?"

Wood chips filled the air as sweaty korlak in work aprons chopped at the logs. Anika watched korlak build bows and arrows. "Those green bows will warp. They should use seasoned wood for that."

Tyric said, "They must anticipate war soon. All more reason we should be back to the castle."

Anika nodded.

The roar of flames doused any sound of the axes on the longs.

"I count nearly fifty korlak working. More in support. More in the forest yet." Tyric gripped the handle of his ax then thought better and left it holstered. "Come this way." Tyric pulled Anika forward. "Crystal, stay hidden here. We will be back."

They moved between piles of wood offal and scrap materials intended for later rework. Freshly made but empty boxes prepared for filling stacked like a hedge before them. Tyric did not worry about trying to be quiet. If the sound of the fires drowned out the axes then he and Anika should remain silent. Their most difficult task was maintaining their camouflage.

A wide space extended from the containers they hid behind to stacks of finished boxed weapons. In the middle of the space stood a huge korlak bow maker shaving wood on a wide bench. The korlak's body was marked with ornate black tattoos. It focused on fine finishing details. Like a work of art. They watched him. If they moved closer to the stack of finished boxes, they would go from a relatively safe hiding spot directly into the sight of this powerful creature.

Anika whispered, "He is marked like you." She

pushed at Tyric's wrist showing the edge of the first tattoo he received during his training.

"Wizard forges. Weapons of war."

The korlak stopped and scrutinized the bow tips. It turned and cupped one hand at the side of its fanged mouth and emitted a shrill whistle that cut through the noise of the clearing. Another korlak looked from a tent. The other workers all looked too. The office korlak waved and went back in, only to exit with a bound book and wearing a cloak. Tattoos marked this korlak like the blacksmith but it wore a wizard's cloak adorned with vivid symbols of fiendish demons.

The korlak wizard and the bow maker worked with the polished bow. They finished wrapping the limbs and handle with ornate threads. They carved special symbols on the limbs. Then the wizard turned pages in the book. It held the book with one hand gesturing at the bow and spoke magic. A purple fog engulfed the weapon punctuated by flashes of light. The wizard finished and closed the book. The purple fog dispersed, leaving glowing orange runes along the length of the bow. The runes faded and a fine black etching remained. The bow maker used a stiff cable and strung the bow. It dry drew the bow back. Tyric saw how much power coiled in the bow. If fired in battle the arrow from it could pierce many armored bodies. Nodding to the wizard, the korlak took out a worn rag. He spit on the bow and polished it before handing it to the wizard.

The wizard took the bow and the book back to its office. The bow maker took another chunk of wood from a stack, put it onto its work table, and began the process again.

Tyric whispered, "Magic weapons sufficient for an army."

"We need to stop them!" Anika said.

"How are we going to do that? Too many."

"We could destroy the wizard's books."

Tyric agreed, "That could slow them."

Anika looked around the clearing, "Follow me." She moved among all the debris and raw materials. Tyric saw how unorganized the korlak kept the work site. He saw how that unorganized chaos helped them now. Anika kept to the shadows and quieter areas. They paused to ensure their movements remained undetected. None of the other workers made artifacts of power, nor did they see other wizards. The other workers cut out and assembled shield bodies, wagon parts, and other items – strong and well designed but without the deep magic.

Anika asked, "How many other weapons sit bound in crates ready for transport? What is this war?" They crept to the tent and lay on the ground hidden by a rough pile of knots cut out of the timber. Tyric lifted the tent's lower edge. Inside they saw the wizard standing at a small desk writing carefully in a book. Two similar books to the one used to make the bow sat on the top of a field book case. Several sheets of other papers lay open on the books.

The far side of the tent had an enormous bed with two women chained to it and who wore only slips of clothes. The korlak wizard stepped away from the standing desk and to the nearest woman. She cowered but the korlak gripped her wrist and pulled her off the bed to her feet. The wizard held her arm high and licked her shoulder, "Oh, you humans are so soft and tasty. You should tell me where the others hide and I'll let you live. Otherwise," he licked her neck, "Hmmm. So tasty."

Tyric pushed under the tent and stood with his ax tightly in hand. In two long strides, Tyric was at the bed and his first ax swing sheared the chains of the first prisoner, the second swing sunk through the chain of the other and gouged through the bed post. "Run, don't stop until you get to the castle," he said to the women.

The wizard shot two bolts of lightning at Tyric. He felt the electricity run across his armor and fade. Tyric smiled. He came at the wizard with a powerful stroke. Wine goblets and papers exploded in a fiery inferno from a miss-directed spell. The wizard fell to the ground – split in two with its intestines spilling across the ground.

Tyric and Anika looked for the magic books and found them scattered on the floor. They kicked the books into the fires. The covers crackled and curled then thin wisps of something began oozing from between the pages. Tyric used his ax to shove the books further into the fires and they stepped back, not sure what would happen with the magic. All remained quietly unchanged. They slipped under the tent and Anika lead Tyric back to the dragon.

The bow maker whistled for the wizard. When the wizard did not appear, the bow maker trudged toward the tent.

"We need to go."

Chapter XX: Wizard in the Wood

Tyric and Anika climbed down a small hill rimmed with boulders. Tyric turned and grabbed Anika's wrist.

Eight figures stood across the hill behind them. "You have been a difficult quarry through this forest." Rulvog said, moving closer while the others raised their crossbows. "A dragon now travels with you." His face wrinkled up as if he smelled a bad odor that accentuated the scars of his old sword wound that crossed his face, "At least it's a small one." They all wore black leather armor but reinforced with riveted steel scales.

"Our wizards have tracked you but somehow your path remained elusive."

Anika moved closer to Tyric, whispering, "Rubied Assassins, some from the castle guard."

Tyric nodded in agreement.

"Of course, having an assassin of your own might aid in improving your discretion."

Anika taunted, "Or fools follow us."

"Before you think about challenging my men we have you surrounded. And the crossbow bolts are coated with darkling fish blood." He shrugged, "Just for added excitement." His scarred lips parted with a grin of rotted teeth, "Men, fire at will."

Well oiled crossbow strings tugged at their bolts setting them into flight. Tyric and Anika dropped behind a rock. Other assassins appeared from behind the trees to either side and fired their bows. Tyric's thoughts darted to his gem, he put up an iron shield wall, and the bolts impinged the magic.

Rulvog said, "I don't like to dress up like a wizard. Too conspicuous. Nor tell that fool Prince Elraf." His hand swirled with a streak of flame that he flung at Tyric and Anika.

The dragon slipped over the rock and took the force of the magic. The fire absorbed into the dragon's skin. Tyric saw the dragon's bright skin dull and then a thin split opened up along each side of the dragon. It wiggled out leaving the husk of its skin, now clean and larger. The assassin wizard paused. The crossbow team clanked their crossbows as they quickly stretched the cables back. One of the assassins slipped with his bolt and stuck himself with the pointed tip. The assassin pitched back in convulsions and death. Rulvog shrugged and returned his attention to Tyric and Anika.

Anika ran directly at Rulvog with a dagger in each of her hands.

Tyric rotated his shield, added a second one, and concentrated on moving the shields so the walls traveled with them as they came at the wizard. Crystal lunged forward ahead of them, absorbing lightning arcs the frightened wizard recklessly cast at them. Tyric could see Crystal thicken but not as she did from the larger fire spell the wizard had cast.

Crystal bumped the wizard to knock him to the ground and Anika struck him with her daggers. The ground around them filled with crossbow bolts. Some of the bolts struck the dragon but bounced off her natural armor-tough skin. Tyric saw an assassin move behind them and fired his crossbow at them between Tyric's shields. He reflexively twisted them in his mind. The walls responded by rotating around. Tyric said, "Anika, stay behind the dragon." He rushed toward the assassin that just fired on him, spinning his shields faster and faster as he came at the assassin. Other crossbow bolts struck his shields, everything around him blinking in and out of his sight but the spin increased. He swung his ax, the shields halting as his ax went through the open space and hit the assassin, splitting his crossbow and wildly firing the bolt. He went after the assassins nearest him with his spinning shields. Their weapons struck the shields or his ax as the protective ring halted. One assassin leaned through the gap to strike at Tyric when the shields spun up and the shields cut through the assassin's body.

Tyric said to Anika when all the assassins lay dead, "They remained brave and did not flee."

"Training. As well as fear to return after a failed mission. Consequences." She shoved her daggers into their sheaths and tipped her head, "The castle should not be too much further."

Explosions rained down through the trees. The forest burned around them. Korlak ringed the edge of the darkness.

"Look at how many eyes are out there!" Anika said, pointing with her sword.

Tyric raised himself above the side of Crystal that wrapped them against the heat, "They stand on all sides of us. Korlak and elves both."

"I don't see any breaks between their numbers."

Another streak of fire left the wizard's hands and struck against the trees over Tyric and Anika, raining burning bits of limbs upon them. The wizard burst purple lightning that exploded stone and soil in fits of energy as it wiggled toward them.

Korlak cranked down a just completed catapult with its load of wood and rock debris. A second catapult released its contents into the air.

"Move!" Tyric pushed across the snarling brambles, Anika and the dragon behind him. The first catapult rotated around tracking Tyric. Then it released. Tyric and Anika dove behind a tree trunk. The rocks slammed into the thick trunk, chipping body sized chunks of wood and bark from it.

The second catapult fired. The rock hurled forward at the sheltering tree. As the rock reached its zenith, the elven wizard waved her hand and the rock exploded in a powerful wave of shrapnel. The blast shredded the trunk, the wood fibers splayed out as the top of the tree toppled down at Tyric and Anika. Tyric pushed his mind into his gem and a heavy steel shield protected them from the falling wood. They watched how the weight of the tree pressed the shield down into the soil. Tyric modified the edge of his shield so they could crawl free.

"I cannot believe how the forest has been cut down to build all those catapults."

"More wood has been removed than is here."

"Have we been gone for months?"

"No, just many workers."

"I wondered how a dragon could learn of a leadership change at the castle but this is not difficult to understand when seeing it."

A purple storm coalesced at the far side of the clearing. The powerful wizard King Frael stood on a stump of a tree that had been many feet thick but now only a scattered pile of its discarded top and the stump remained.

A shadow crossed the clearing, looping around. The dark blot gave Tyric the prickly sensation a rabbit has when hunted under a hawk's shadow. The dragon arched around and landed at another corner of the clearing that remained free of korlak and elves.

King Frael screeched, raising his arms. Thunder toiled about the clearing, electrifying the air with violent fingers, thrashing through the mists of a storm.

The dragon swept up winds of her own with her wings, testing in each direction how King Frael's shifted, and matching force with force, keeping King Frael's winds from circling, turning, and spiraling into a cyclone. Tyric and Anika's bodies and clothes fluttered like birds in a storm. King Frael reached into the swirling dust and coiled it into a sooty black beast that darkened the more King Frael's magic solidified it. The thing launched itself forward with six sturdy arms. Two hands squirmed at each end of these arms, moving it with the fluidity of a telnak through the snows, the quickness of fire through dry timber. Then it sprang from its fingertips to the dragon's throat. The dragon put up a magic barrier and the strangler landed heavily against the magic. She let magic pour from her talons like the silky sands along an ocean. The magic poured into a white mountain dog that leaped at the strangler. Purple lightning snapped down, crackling furiously. The dragon struck power down her talons, snatching each violent length in her grip, drawing them like wires from the air. Then weaving their power together into another larger golden wall of power. The white dog lashed its head into the strangler gouging the creature's scaly body until the dog's jaws clamped on an arm. The dog whipped the strangler up and bashed it against a rock protruding out of the twisted wreckage of felled trees. The strangler still struggled in the dog's grip. The dog whipped the strangler against the rock a second time and the strangler fell silent.

King Frael brought his Shadow Staff higher completing a purple ball and he watched the mountain dog sprint across the clearing for him. King Frael let go of the staff, allowing it to balance perfectly in the air as he pointed at the running dog. The white dog burst into flames and fell to the ground in a smoking ruin. The purple orb floated across the clearing, meeting the dragon's golden wall. The two objects hesitated as if preparing for a kiss. Then both expanded, embracing and engulfing each other along with the dragon and the wizard.

Tyric could only see points of power through the swirling gold and violet marking the positions of the dragon and the wizard. Crystal turned from the edge of the wood and ran forward of Tyric and Anika until she stood at the swirling cauldron's edge. Tyric ordered, "Crystal, get back with us –" He watched swirling clouds covering the dragon and the wizard bleed tendrils of colored smoke that sucked into Crystal. He watched the young dragon expand, her skin split and she expanded again. The Shadow Staff spewed inky strength into the field. The dragon pushed brilliant light against the flaying darkness. King Frael retaliated with a greater force. Pain scorched the dragon's thoughts, her mind shuddered, the darkness taking more ground at each glance. The dragon fought back, struggling against the increasing force from the wizard. Tyric saw the dragon slipping. The dragon's magic surged up and down in wild bursts. He watched as she stumbled and became only a point of energy fading away leaving the dragon visible, with shredded bloody wounds. Light and dark spirals of purple and pale white swept in a deadly fog between the dragon and the wizard.

The dragon reeled, hypnotized by the configurations pounding against her magic, yet more weakened by the wizard's strikes. The darkness deepened until it clamped upon the dragon and gnawed upon her. "No!" Tyric yelled, his gem fusing with his thoughts, ruin striking though his emotions. Darkness stabbed at his mind. Waves of pain, sadness, and sorrow spilled through Tyric from the dragon. He staggered. He saw the other creatures stumbling to stay upright as if an earthquake struck the world. Tattered images of her wounds ripped through his mind. Helplessness and disorientation consumed him in the glowing darkness.

Crystal reached through the darkness so bright she burned through Tyric's eyes from his mind. King Frael spread his power at the young dragon. Tyric pushed his shield wall out and protected Crystal against the magic. He felt the power vibrating against his gem's magic but it held. Tyric pulled at his mind and his gem amid the barrage of wizard magic hitting the wall in front of Crystal, and the tendrils of smoke that raced at him. Tyric lashed together another shield and pushed it at the mother dragon.

    His shield came too late.

    Tyric and Crystal ran from the edge of the clearing, Anika behind them, more wary of the wizard that swayed with the staff he held, readying a purple storm overhead.

    Tyric dropped to his knees, his helmet sliding from his slack fingers, "She can't be dead!" He pressed his hands against the dragon's body. Nothing stirred. The fire in her eyes flickered and faded. "What am I to do?"

    Crystal barked in baleful sorrow that came down to a roaring growl. The dragon whipped around and stalked toward the wizard in revenge.

    Tyric ordered, "Back to the woods, you are not safe here." He pulled at his ax, "I will avenge your mother." The dragon growled but nodded at Tyric's command and pulled away. The dragon backed to the edge of the clearing, keeping watch over Tyric and the wizard.

    Tyric ran at the wizard.

    "You will need my help." Tyric spun at Anika's words.

    "No. I don't want to worry about you. To the woods with the dragon."

Anika said, "I'm not sitting on the side while you die here."

"I won't."

"You need my sword."

"I need you to protect the dragon."

"The dragon will be fine as long as she stays there – and you survive."

"As will you. I ... I can't see you killed." The wizard's clouds darkened the whole wood around them. Tyric's eyes flamed and his teeth clenched feeling the wizard energy rising around them.

"– You won't. And I won't leave you to fight the wizard on your own."

"Please stay. I have to attack," Tyric sprinted toward the wizard.

Anika ran after him with her sword drawn, "Tyric!"

Tyric pushed a shield over her and it sunk into the ground. Tyric could hear her banging at the inside of the shield with her sword. He sprinted for the wizard.

The wizard shifted, swinging his arms around. Jagged forking lightning reached for Tyric from the scratching sky. He jumped as the energy struck the soil bursting in an explosion beside him. He spun to the other side as an electric finger reached for him. The energy pulled at the torn twigs discarded in front of him and wiggled along all the branches exploding in a flash of fire that knocked him back to the ground. Clods of soil rained upon him as he gripped the ground to right himself and charge ahead. The wizard laughed. The storm reached for Tyric again. Tyric put his hand out and a shield expanded before and over him, sunk firmly into the grounding soil. The energy struck the shield and followed the path into the soil that Tyric provided. His shield faded as he gained his feet and came nearer the wizard with his ax raised.

Elves wearing armor made in the korlak forges surrounded Tyric's shield protecting Anika. They put away their weapons and slipped shovels from their packs. The elves knelt shoulder to shoulder and dug around the edges of the shell. Other elves brought timbers and jacks.

Korlak surged from the woods and surrounded the dragon. Crystal snapped her jaws at the first of them. She kicked another with her hind foot breaking its spine. Her tail lashed out, clenching around the neck of another that she lifted up and threw into the larger rushing horde.

The wizard spun his arm around and pitched a flaming orb at Tyric. Tyric's thoughts dipped through his gem and the magic dispersed as it hit him. Tyric reached the surprised wizard and struck his ax against his robes.

The wizard's robe hardened where the ax blade contacted it like a stone wall. Tyric struck again but the wizard's robe hardened and protected him. The wizard swung his staff at Tyric. The bristling spines along the staff raked across his armor, gouging the metal, tearing at his flesh between the weaker armor joints and his muscle below.

Tyric crashed his ax into the staff, shattering several spines and stopping the wizard's next blow. He back handed his weapon into the wizard and the robe again made itself ridged and stopped his attack.

The elves dug below the bottom of Anika's shield. They positioned timbers and levered up the edge of the shield. The front row of digging elves fell back and fresh elves stepped into the deepening moat around Anika. Their digging work quickened. Nipped chunks of tree roots rolled down the dirt piles, black along their length but the severed ends shown pure white. They brought other timbers forward and added to the work. Anika stayed low and far back at the edge of the shield that still contacted the soil. Her fingers clenched the grip of her sword and watched the elves chew away at the dirt. She knew Tyric thought her safe here and would not think to rescue her.

The korlak beat their swords against the dragon but nothing they had pierced the dragon's skin. Crystal crushed several in her jaws. She kicked away others with her feet and stabbed another with the slim end of her tail or wrapped it around the neck of another. It threw them against a nearby tree trunk. The korlak mass parted and a pair of elite korlak fighters came forward. They each used two swords, a short and a long, wore lightweight black armor with violet war paint splashed across their faces and chests.

Crystal lashed her tail around another korlak getting too close and whipped the body into the two that approached her with so much confidence. They both stepped aside and the body passed between them. Then they charged at the dragon, their swords a blur around them.

Tyric struck the wizard with his ax and again the magical carapace protected the wizard. He saw how the robe welded the wizard in place while it protected him.

He struck again lighter and faster. The lightning fingers reached for Tyric. He spun up a shield and blocked the lightning but during his distraction, the wizard lifted something out of the ground with the tip of his staff. A flaming fist sunk pointed talons into a tree root and pulled the rest of the creature up through the soil.

Crystal snaked her tail around the legs of another korlak and swung the body at the two approaching her. The first ducked and the second swung his sword and sliced through the korlak and its armor in a single strong stroke. The dragon released the remains of the body to strike into another group of korlak standing ready. Crystal squared her body before them and readied her talons for whichever approached her first. Crystal struck at the korlak. The korlak stabbed with its sword and pierced the dragon's foot. The second sliced at her lower leg. The dragon bellowed at the wounds. She knew they wielded magic swords.

Anika batted at the first of the elven swords that groped for her. The digging continued. Timbers propped the device up and they came for her.

The black creature looked like a giant korlak but more twisted and with flames scorching down its arms. It swept a mace at Tyric, connecting with his arm in a solid strike that bent the blacksmith sideways and knocked him to the ground. Tyric's arm felt numb and as responsive as the black roots the elves tossed upon the dirt piles. His mind let loose of Anika's shield as he rolled to avoid another strike from the mace that sunk into the leaf bed as easily as swamp muck.

Crystal brought her tail around and stabbed into the nearest korlak where the tip nicked into the space between helmet and its shoulder armor. She hooked the end of her tail and ripped the throat of the korlak from it. The second korlak snatched the falling long sword from it and spun, sinking both blades into the dragon's chest.

The shield snapped away leaving Anika crouching on a tuft of undisturbed dirt and the timbers crawling with elves. She sprang off her lump of dirt, over the heads of the nearest elf climbing from the trench, and landed on the discarded dirt pile. She sunk to her knees in the dirt and fought at freeing her feet and getting over the soft mound. The elves dropped their shovels, freed their weapons, and charged her.

The dragon reeled at the pain. She arched her back, standing on her hind legs and waving her front talons at the stabbing pain. The korlak released one sword and snatched a dagger from its belt and cut along the dragon's ankle as those talons tried brushing the swords away.

New pain raked along the dragon's leg. Her other front claw clamped around the korlak's chest. The korlak twisted its sword and pulled it free, widening the wound. Crystal rolled onto her back, brought her rear claws up, and dug them in just below her grip on the korlak's chest. Her rear talons ripped into the korlak and sliced through it. The dead korlak hung like a tattered flag from the dragon's front claw until she dropped the bloody body. The pain of the other sword still burned in her chest. She brought her tail to the sword, lashed it around the handle, and yanked it free. The other korlak launched at her with ropes, chains, and the magic daggers they found upon the ground.

Anika kicked herself onto her back and rolled down the far side of the dirt pile. When she felt the firmer soil of the forest floor, she stood and launched herself into the converging elves. Her sword struck down the first three.

Crystal hugged one of her claws against her wounds trying to make the bleeding stop. She swung her tail at the first row of korlak approaching. The blade her tail wrapped sliced through the armor and korlak of that first row. The sword cut through the chains and ropes they carried. Other korlak raced at her from behind. She whirled and sliced through them. The other korlak paused.

The flaming demon struck at Tyric with long rake-like claws that pointed forward from the backs of its fists. Tyric dropped to the ground and rolled aside to avoid its punch. The fist slammed into the leaf cover, billowing up the drier leaves. The second fist swung the mace at him. Tyric matched the mace swing with his ax, deflecting the heavy ball across the face of his ax and into the ground next to Tyric.

Tyric brought his ax up and cut into the arm of the demon. The forge fire hot flames running along its arms burned Tyric. Any leather on his armor smoldered and he turned his face away from the intense heat. He chopped blindly at the stout thigh. His ax struck deep and hard. Tyric turned his body in the direction to loosen the ax, yank it free, and struck again into the thigh bone. The demon pushed the mace at Tyric, banging into his chest armor and holding him down. Tyric pushed at the ground with his arms and legs and could not free himself. The demon pressed harder and Tyric felt his armor flexing into his chest.

"Pinned down like an insect," said the wizard. "You seem impervious to direct magic but not to beasts I can summon. Like that dragon absorbing my magic because it is young." The wizard curled his eyes up into his head and lashed out with energy from his hands that charged through the air timed with a lightning strike from the sky to hit the dragon. The magic knocked the dragon back, rolled her over and against a tree. He saw how the dragon shimmered and grew, absorbing the magic. The dragon rolled to her legs, the splitting skin falling from her in shattered strips because the growth came so fast. This time her full grown body stretched out magnificent wings as her graceful neck arched up. Now he understood she could not absorb more magic. New magic would wound the dragon. He grinned. "She is more dangerous but also more vulnerable." Korlak came again at the dragon as the wizard pushed magic against her. Tyric dug his mind through his gem and built a small shield before the dragon. The wizard remained too fast for Tyric when he moved his arms at Anika across the shattered wood. Anika froze in place in front of elves about to strike her. Unimpeded, the elves stabbed into her unmoving form. The wizard released her and she fell to the ground, "But then the simplest magic can stop a traitorous assassin."

The demon leaned its burning face toward Tyric's, moaning in glee. Tyric tried twisting away from the demon while he increased the shield before the dragon. The demon struck its fist at Tyric's head, jarring his mind and tossing off the dragon's shield. The magic struck the dragon and flung her back. The sword flipped through the tree-tops and struck a back-rank korlak then into the ground and out of sight as if it cut through the choppy surface of a violent lake. The lightning from the sky gouged into the dragon while the other energy appeared to melt her skin. The dragon writhed upon the ground. The korlak converged with their magic daggers and sliced into the sides of the wounded dragon.

Searing burns chewed into Tyric's body from the demon that leaned closer. What might be a grin upon its face or just the rankled crooked teeth that pass for a smile in the demon world from which it came, chortled over him. Tyric's breath crushed out of him as the demon's leer widened and he could only think, *I could not save them!* Despair charred his mind into floating blackened bits that scattered upon the breeze of desperation. He picked at the broken shards and looked through their sharp edges until the pain inflicted upon his body by the demon pulled him from it. He thought deep and created a shield that he put above him and through the menacing demon. The demon pieces fell away. Tyric rolled to his knees and pushed himself to his feet. His breath came in slow, painful draws. His eyes saw the korlak hacking into the dragon and the elves stabbing Anika's body. He split two shields and covered both of them in protective shells. He brought his eyes to the wizard's, "A mistake."

"No, it's your mistake."

King Frael, entwined in his flurry of robes, stood stiffly on the fractured tree stump. The Shadow Staff held loosely between his hands.

Tyric created another shield that bisected the wizard. He watched the hiss of the field form from nothingness but the wizard waved the staff and Tyric's shield dispersed. He tried again and the wizard canceled it with the staff's magic. The wizard laughed. He thumped the staff on the ground. A crack opened in the forest floor and traveled toward Tyric. "A crack in the world might swallow you yet."

Tyric leaped aside. The crack turned and wiggled toward him. Another demon climbed up from the bottom of the crack that continued orienting itself at Tyric as he ran to stay ahead of it. The crack cornered Tyric and as it approached, threatening to swallow him into the deep soil, he made a shield that spanned the wide gorge and ran to the far side.

Thunder toiled about the clearing, electrifying the air with violent fingers, thrashing through the mists of the wizard's storm. The wizard's winds circled and spiraled into a cyclone. The leaves kicked up from the ground to flutter like a bird in the storm. The sooty black beast of a strangler propelled itself at Tyric on its six sturdy arms. It sprang from its fingertips to Tyric's throat. Tyric made a shield and the strangler landed heavily against it. Purple lightning snapped through the air. Tyric canceled his shield as his ax swing came through it and struck the strangler with his full force.

The demon's fiery hand locked on Tyric's ankle and it pulled itself out of the crack in the world to the forest floor. Loose leaves that stirred in the air or the drier ones on the ground flared in the presence of the demon. The demon threw him down. An inky strength coiled around the wizard's staff and against Tyric that darkened everything. Tyric did not feel the ground. He continued falling and guessed the demon had tossed him into the open ground. Tyric put down a long shield that might span the widest crack. He struck the softened iron hard. He rolled to his back to ease the widening pain across his chest. He tried getting light from his gem. It only flickered against the night. He put more of his thoughts into the gem to get it to shine brighter.

A bright light enveloped Tyric's eyes. Somehow he knew the light came not from around him but from inside the gem. Out of that light came a regal King in flowing wizard robes. A sword dangled from his hand at the end of a weary arm. Once polished plate armor showed the battered abuse of too many battles. He leaned on a gnarled staff that glowed brightly. He did not appear young nor old – just fatigued through his bones. He said in comforting tones, "I am Aleron and you must pull together your siblings. They already seek you. Only by reuniting the family will you have the power to resist the Shadow Wizard." He reached forward, his sword vanishing from his hand. "You and your brothers and sisters will need to call me from the grave to resist the evil." He faded as his voice dispersed, "You have a great roll ahead in this war. The road ahead is as hard as any anvil, Tyric, my son."

Tyric found himself in the darkness again. His mind raced at what the vision meant. He knew he could ponder that later, if he survived the wizard. He got to his feet and listened. He heard the demon searching for him and the buffeting winds of magic around the wizard. Tyric modified his shield to continue under his footsteps while he approached the wizard. He raised his ax and swung it at the wizard.

The demon bashed its mace at Tyric, knocking him away. Darkness strove at his mind; the only light was his, all else remained so black! The power about him wrapped like a curtain so he could not locate anything. His body did not hit the ground. He spun in emptiness. He realized he must be deep down a crevice already. He expanded a shield under him and kept making it wider until he felt friction and it stopped his fall.

Tyric stood in the darkness and the quiet with his hands searching the nearest wall. No crevices appeared in the hard stone stacked layer upon layer up the walls. He found his pack missing along with the ropes attached to it, all cut from him in the fight. He bent his neck and propped his head against the wall, despair taking hold of him again. Then he felt a buzzing in the wall and it moved. He felt the crack closing! Could his shield keep the walls from crushing him? He did not want to try, but how to get out of here? He tried putting another shield above the one he stood on and climbed onto it. Then he put one slightly higher. He placed shields like steps, fading away those below as he made new ones. He could still sense that the ones he put around Anika and the dragon remained in place. He climbed higher on his steps. The wall moved and he did not know how far away the other wall remained. His steps quickened.

A mace clanged on his shield step. Tyric moved to the side and struck with his ax. He felt the resistance of flesh and armor and bone as the weapon cut through the creature's leg. Tyric stepped onto another shield and his ax cut deep into the side of the demon. The demon swung its mace around and hit Tyric's side lifting him up and throwing him against the wizard. Tyric slid down the wizard's robe that had hardened into armor.

The wizard struck at Tyric with his staff. Tyric's ax froze the wizard's arm when the robe solidified and protected the wizard from his weapon. Tyric hit him again in another location and another. Tyric struck the wizard and kept him fixed upon the stump.

Tyric's mind flashed on his last view of Anika crumpled on the ground before the korlak. Maddened, he swung his ax hard and high into the wizard's throat. The ax struck into the gap in the wizard's hood and cut through the wizard's neck. The blow continued into the inside of the cloak and the magic shattered like glass. The wizard's head bounded into the brush and a cloud of black shards exploded before Tyric, raking his armor and throwing him down. The cracks in the ground vanished with the darkness while the demon spun to the depths from which the wizard had summoned it. The korlak broke into confusing fights among themselves and lashed out at the elves that a moment before were their allies. The elves scattered in fear and fled into the forest followed by chaotic groups of grinning korlak, coordination broken with their leader dead.

"You need to live, Anika." Tyric knelt by her side, his hands upon her. She seemed so frail and broken he feared she might be dead. He placed his hand against her heart. He closed his eyes and pushed his mind through his gem. He saw the blackness of her wounds and wove her flesh together until her body glowed under his hands. His own body restored as he helped her.

Anika's hand reached up and touched Tyric's face, her voice warm as she said, "I love you."

Tyric's eyes pooled into hers, "Not more than I love you."

She smiled, "Perhaps."

Tyric jerked his head away as he rose to his feet, "But I must see to Crystal."

Anika stood on wobbly legs and saw the unmoving dragon, saying after Tyric, "You can heal her?"

"Not if she is already dead –"

Chapter XXI: The Alliance

The lush greens and browns of the forest sparkled with mountain flowers. The glittery spires atop the silver-white walls of the castle appeared as they left the edge of the forest. The wind blew hard against them, shredding their hair and burnishing their cheeks. Tyric felt the undulations of the powerful wing muscles pulling across the dragon's frame below them. He had fashioned a workable saddle so he and Anika did not fall off the dragon but he knew they would need something better later. With his shop, he could fabricate it easily and finely. Anika tapped his shoulder and pointed to the courtyard.

Tyric nudged Crystal and the dragon banked and circled. Her massive shadow curled across the castle battlements and towers. Tyric could feel the fear of those below that looked up and saw the dragon gliding down toward them. The guard scampered for cover and their weapons. Tyric saw the guards relied on their training to hold their crossbows aimed at the dragon from the battlements.

Crystal landed in the empty courtyard. The tired red tongue of the carpet that normally lay in welcome through the great doorway was absent from the steps. The guard had closed and barred the great doors to the throne room.

Tyric slipped down the dragon's side with Anika and they walked to the massive doors. Tyric thumped his ax handle against the wood. "I wish to speak with the King."

Tyric waited.

"You better knock again," Anika said. "They had enough time to walk back and forth to the King. Unless they are hiding."

"I don't think Prince Elraf, or rather King Elraf, would hide."

"Is he King yet?"

Tyric shrugged, "We spent a few days with Crystal learning to fly. Quite possible and necessary." Tyric looked at the dragon that waited unblinking in the courtyard. Her wings tucked tight against herself but ready to launch. "Remind me not to do that again."

Anika smiled, "You had fun except for that one flip you nearly fell."

"And why we have the saddle now," Tyric said.

Crystal snorted.

Tyric raised his ax and banged the handle against the door. He liked how the wood handle bounced off the planks that made up the door, revealing their respective solid construction. He heard motion behind the portals and then one of the two doors cracked open.

King Elraf came through the narrow opening and stood alone. "My advisors suggested I have the whole guard down here before I talk with you. Others suggested I arrest you for your crimes."

Tyric said, "We thought the dragon might deter such issues."

"Yes. You were correct." The elf nodded. "The dragon proves my father's stories were more than children's entertainment. May I look at it?"

"Her," Anika said. "Her name is Crystal."

The elf tipped his head toward the dragon, "May I look at the dragon Crystal? I have never seen one."

Tyric waved his hand toward the dragon. The bright sunshine sparkled along the dragon's platinum skin. "We returned because your father sent me on the errand to find the dragon's egg and return it to its mother. We did and she hatched the egg."

"Then my brother tried to kill you and both dragons."

"So you know what happened?"

"Yes." King Elraf surveyed the dragon's form. "Powerful. Frightening. I see why the old stories talked of them with such reverence and fear. One cannot be but in awe." King Elraf turned to Tyric, "You could have killed me in the forest when I pursued you for a crime that I've since discovered you did not commit."

"I escaped without a need to do that."

King Elraf sighed, "In the few days since my brother's death I've found so many new truths. He was an administrator for the Rubied Assassins and he sought wizardry powers more unrestrained than a Snowy Elf, leading him into the dark magic of a Shadow Staff. Even dealing the kingdom for it. The korlak are on the move and old magic from the old war is returning. So I find myself King of a kingdom at the edge of a new war. Bad times are ahead – we need strong alliances, we need strong people. We need the

Son of Aleron –"

"How do you know that?"

"Old elven stories. How do you think a dragon's egg hidden in Emperor's Keep remained a secret from king to king through the last thousand years? Who would have given them the secret?"

Anika said, "Aleron."

"Aleron could see the future. A dire future filled with darkness and danger. Somehow, he willed his children into that far future because they would be called upon to save the land. He could have used the same magic to put them in quiet peaceful days. Instead, he chose the most dangerous time imaginable, at the cusp of the Shadow Wizard's return. The dragon and reports of what you did on the field of battle against my brother only convinced me." Prince Elraf knelt down before the human. "Tyric, Son of Aleron, I pledge the whole of the Enkarian Kingdom to you in this coming war."

Tyric looked from the resting dragon, to Anika anxious on her toes, and then back to the King. He clasped the King's hand in agreement.

Where will this alliance lead us?

THE END

Coming Soon!

Rise Of The Crimson Knights

The forests are burning and the cities are falling as the might of the Shadow Wizard extends darkness across the land. Fearsome monsters forgotten to legend and myth have returned to terrorize the world. The Korlak, strengthened by a skeleton army created in secret over centuries, attack the East and grind their way West, driving peace and the populace toward certain doom at the Gelvorian Rift. Death feeds upon the chaos as thieves and opportunistic rogues take from the weak and the vulnerable ahead of the storm.

Leaving nothing to chance, the Shadow Wizard trained an elite group of hunters to stalk the Children of Aleron, but already strife exists between the heroes. Can they learn to work together to heal their dissension and build trust? Can they overcome the treachery of those they once knew as friends and those they hoped were allies? Who will remain to vanquish the rapacious hunger of the Shadow Wizard? Or will night fall over the land, slipping hope into oppression and death?

Find out in <u>RISE OF THE CRIMSON KNIGHTS</u>, Book 1 of the *Crimson Furl Trilogy*.

A Personal Note from the Author

Thank you for reading! If you enjoyed this novel then please visit the book on-line and leave a review to encourage others to take a chance with the characters in this Epic tale. I rely on word of mouth and your kind words mean a lot to me!

I blog about my writing projects at http://jgordonsmith.com where I post updates and events. Join my email list at my website and you'll get notified when new titles are published. I hope to see you there!

The Gemstone Series

Book I: The Diamond Coronal
Book II: The Black Jewel
Book III: The Fire Gem
Book IV: The Blue Crystal

The four books of the Gemstone Series can be read in any order as the events occur along the parallel paths of each main character. The Crimson Furl Trilogy occurs at the end of the first four books taking all the main characters and their powers to save the land from the Shadow Wizard.

<u>The Diamond Coronal</u>
Book I of the Gemstone Series

"No!" Maurius cried hoarsely as Dorran's body crumpled to the bloody ground. The lieutenant spun in the crunching gravel path and, with a grin of triumph, he ran toward Maurius – intent upon another kill –
The wizard Maurius seeks a mysterious staff named the Gnarled Burner, blamed for the demise of the inquisitive Snowy Elves a thousand years ago. What begins as a leisurely academic quest into the snow and ice covered Northern Mountains quickly turns into a sprint through the arctic cold to find the staff before it falls into evil hands. Can Maurius avoid the Rubied Assassins that attack him wherever he goes? Will he prevail against creatures nearly forgotten in myth that

eerily haunt him behind every stone and hill? What ancient evil awoke bringing war to the land with the vengeance of old dragons? And what dangerous Destiny lurks in the Diamond he carries, has always carried, yet does not know from where it came?

> The Black Jewel
> Book II of the Gemstone Series

Sylanna's jaw scraped against the rough plastered wall, "You cannot be one of the guardsmen."

"And how did you guess that? Was it my curt accent or my fashionable attire?" His sweaty arm clamped tighter, grinding into her belly, while his other hand held a long dagger against her throat. Sylanna's mind scattered. She had not even heard him approach!

The talented thief Sylanna flees to a remote monastery after she is attacked by the Rubied Assassins. But she learns the quiet monastery is anything but silent; pious monks plot against each other, executions and murder are brushed aside, ancient secrets are buried deep under the fortified structure, while the studious leaders supply the brewing War. Will Sylanna survive the monastery and its suspicious monks? Will she escape the Rubied Assassins or will they surprise her behind the monastery's thick walls and wide moat? Who can be a friend and who is secretly an enemy? Even the Black Jewel, a comforting talisman she has carried since childhood, clutches a dangerous Destiny that unwinds as the menace approaches. Can she stop the evil?

<u>The Fire Gem</u>
Book III of the Gemstone Series

Koren stood and slowly turned in the smoky dust from the shattered throne, her swords still ringing from their violence. She growled behind eyes flaming with battlefield ferocity, "We will have no more sitting – We Go To WAR!"

Victory in the violent Kelvin Arena sowed envy and filled the tribal leaders with contempt against the savage warrior Koren. While scarcely believing a human could best the fearsome eight armed kelvin gladiators, they grudgingly gave her blades uneasy respect.

But now strange enemies wielding ancient magic murder whole villages of the mighty kelvin without a breath of resistance. Koren seeks salvation from the magic with the ancient Sword of Aleron – a broken blade scattered across the dangerous Swamps of Kal at the end of the last Great War – and it must be forged anew in the fires that made it. Attacked by nightmarish creatures and pursued by relentless teams of Rubied Assassins can Koren save the kelvin from slaughter? Will treasonous kelvin leaders betray her when confronted by old emotions, ancient enemies, and a War now unearthed? Can she forge the chaotic tribes into a single force to repel the impending menace? And what are the disturbing visions seething within her Fire Gem – an ancient Destiny she cannot escape?

Other Books Written by J Gordon Smith

<u>ZOMBIE TATTOO</u> by J Gordon Smith
The aZure Tribe – Short Story #0.5
(Science Fiction)

"Tell me again how a thirty-eight gun British Frigate came to rest here at the bottom of the world?" A brutal Antarctic wind shook the protective canvas tarp behind Doctor Cooper like the lusty snap of a ghostly sail. "Any guess at what we might find?" But the growling reply of the sectioning saw covered their voices as it gnawed into the black, frozen wood.

The archeology researchers pry into the ancient pirate ship and release a horror hidden in the frozen ice for three hundred years. They might think of warning the world of the virus if not so preoccupied in surviving the tattooed monster that lived in that cold, undead ship – waiting for them …

Zombie Tattoo is a short story that chronicles the beginning and launch of *The aZure Tribe Trilogy*, a shared zombie apocalyptic world. For short stories, <u>Zombie Tattoo</u> is on the longer end of the spectrum approaching 10,000 words, hearkening back to Science Fiction's long love of the short form. Do you dare uncover the tattooed horror that lives within?

<u>ONE NIGHT BURNS</u> by J Gordon Smith

J GORDON SMITH

A Vampires of Livix Novel – Volume 1
(Paranormal Romance)

The front door exploded free of its hinges. Glass and wood shrapnel shattered across the room bouncing from furniture and walls. Garin tucked me protectively behind his body as across the broken threshold strode three snarling vampires. I recognized their leader –

Once Patent Attorney Anna Arkena meets the handsome and intriguing vampire Garin Ramsburgh, a bold Investment Analyst at Draydon Financial, she quickly learns how her life in the small mid-western town of Livix will change.

The Vampires of Livix cringe as these two become close – mixing with vampires always ends badly. But the problems only escalate as outside interests pressure Garin's wealthy family to sell their successful military parts business amid faked financial losses. And international terrorist and militia groups push their own agendas with deadly effectiveness.

Who is behind it all? What do they want? Is this only a spark of a greater fire to come? Will Anna survive the vampires? Can Anna and Garin achieve happiness? Will she find True Love?

Find out in the *Vampires Of Livix* trilogy!

CABERNET ZIN by J Gordon Smith
(New Adult Contemporary Romance)

THE BLUE CRYSTAL

Zachary Steel is a handsome, mid-twenties, stay-at-home father who sacrificed his promising industrial career to make life better for his children. He finds his now sole-bread-winning wife becoming more resentful and vicious and then he learns – unfaithful. He copes with his loveless loss by passionately throwing himself into his small, struggling California winery investment.

Among the Temecula valley vineyards Zack glimpses the promise of love again when he meets Claire touring the wineries with her friends – a captivating and smart young woman working her first job out of business college.

Claire wonders why she finds this married man so charming and desirable and worries she is only a quickly forgotten fling when she wants so much more of him. Zack is terrified Claire could abandon him and twist his heartache for her into disappointment, sadness, and dark loneliness – especially when he finds she has been keeping a secret from him. Can they cling together through tragedy and strengthen each other against family opposition to their growing relationship? Will they build trust and True Love on top of hot desire among the California vineyards?

Will they find despair ... or happiness?

About the Author

J Gordon Smith began reading Swords & Sorcery novels growing up on a farm in Michigan. The vast array of speculative fiction not only entertained but posed influential ideas impacting the direction of his education, career, and writing.

J Gordon Smith resides in a suburb near Detroit and runs a successful engineering and general business consulting company supporting both local and global corporations involved with producing cars and trucks that you probably own and drive every day.

THE BLUE CRYSTAL